RAIDERS OF THE ROCKIES

STONECROFT SAGA 5

B.N. RUNDELL

WOLFPACK
PUBLISHING
—— EST 2013 ——

WOLFPACK
PUBLISHING
— EST 2013 —

Raiders Of The Rockies

Paperback Edition
Copyright © 2020 B.N. Rundell

Wolfpack Publishing
6032 Wheat Penny Avenue
Las Vegas, NV 89122

wolfpackpublishing.com

Paperback ISBN 978-1-64734-499-3
eBook ISBN 978-1-64734-498-6

RAIDERS OF THE ROCKIES

DEDICATION

There are so many that deserve recognition and thanks. From my loving wife who is always beside me and supportive of me, to the many others that have their hands and minds involved in this work. The editors, the cover designers, the proof readers, and the mastermind that takes it to market, (All at Wolfpack Publishing), all deserving of innumerable accolades, and of course the readers. I only regret that I am unable to shake each hand, look into the eye of each one and say, 'Thank you!' So until that better time when I am able to say it in person, to each and every one of you I say, Thanks so much! You are greatly appreciated!

1 / Winter

The drifting snow stacked against the palisade type wall at the face of the granite monolith, sliding over the long mound of interred berry bushes and obscuring any tracks that marred the simplistic sculpture of white. A buckskin clad, tall, sandy-haired man pushed his way through the door, greeted by shouts of alarm from inside. The slow rising sun had painted the eastern sky with broad strokes of orange, tinting the snow with the reflection. From a distance, the palisaded cabin was unseen beneath the snow-covered megalith that stood as a sentinel over the mouth of the Popo Agie River canyon.

Across the river and below the cabin lay a wide valley. The white expanse marked only by the inverted cone tips of the thirty lodges of the small band of Kuccuntikka Shoshone. The only movement in the stillness of the early morning showed at the lower end of the valley where three young men, clad in heavy buffalo robes, watched over the horse herd of the village. Most of the animals were bedded down within the trees on the lee side of the rocky and timbered foothills of the Wind River Mountains, but a few dug at the snow for some graze.

Inside the cabin, Gabriel Stonecroft stomped his feet to rid his buckskin britches fringe and moccasins of the cold snow, then stepped toward the fireplace and seated himself on his wolf pelt covered chair and propped his cold feet on the hearth. He was watched by his wife, Pale Otter, of the Shoshone, who smiled and laughed at his antics. "Bear's paws are cold?" she asked, giggling a little. Gabe was also known as Spirit Bear, or Claw of the Spirit Bear, or Bear Claw. All were derivatives of the same name that Pale Otter had shortened to 'Bear.' They were soon joined by Ezra Blackwell, or Black Buffalo, the life-long friend of Gabe and his wife, the sister of Pale Otter, Grey Dove. This was the first winter for all the newlyweds and they were enjoying the coziness of the cabin they built into the mouth of the overhanging granite monolith just before winter set in and brought the first deep snow.

Although Gabe and Ezra had started work on their cabin in mid-summer, they were soon joined by the band of Shoshone they had earlier befriended. Within days, the two sisters were paired up with the men and spent most of their time together, learning the language of the different people and becoming better acquainted. And as closeness often does, it soon led to deeper feelings and before the summer ended, both men were joined to their women in a Shoshone ceremony celebrated by the entire village.

For two years, the men had traveled together from Philadelphia down the Ohio River, across the Mississippi, fighting bounty hunters, river pirates, and native tribes, and into the Indian lands known by some as the western wilderness but most often referred to as Spanish Louisiana Territory. Their journey began as the result of a duel between Gabriel Stonecroft and Jason Wilson, the son of a powerful and well-connected but vengeful man. When Jason insulted Gabe's sister, the duel came about and was to be fought according to the Code Duello and the usual agreement between gentlemen. But Jason, as was his character, or lack of it, thought to do things according to his way and missed his stolen shot, but Gabe didn't and Jason died. When Wilson's father put a sizable bounty on Gabe's head, Gabe chose to leave the country to ward off any attack against his widowed father or sister, and his best friend, Ezra would not let him leave alone.

Now the two men, as different as night and day, but bound together by life-long friendship and the bond of brotherhood formed in battle, were brothers in more ways than they ever imagined. Married to sisters, Gabe, a white aristocrat from the city, and Ezra, the son of the pastor of the largest church for coloreds in Philadelphia and his wife, known as Black-Irish for her heritage and color, were truly brothers fulfilling their long held dream of exploring the uncharted wilderness of what was known as Spanish Louisiana or French Louisiana, depending on who was in power at the time. The Rocky Mountains had been their primary goal, and now they had built a home at the base of the Wind River Mountain Range right in the middle of the Rockies.

Gabe looked at his smiling wife, always enamored by the beauty of the Shoshone woman, large dark eyes whose deep pools told of an insatiable curiosity for knowledge, long black hair that draped over her shoulders and shone even in the dark of night. Her high cheekbones accented her eyes and her pouty lips that whispered his name bathed in love. He asked, "How 'bout giving my feet a massage, they're mighty cold!" he grinned as he spoke, knowing touching his feet took all her resolve.

"That fire will do you more good than any massage I can give," she responded. "I do not think you want me touching your stinking feet before I fix your breakfast!"

Gabe chuckled, looked at Ezra, "Does Grey Dove treat you like that?"

Ezra laughed, "Umm, no sir! She loves me and everything about me!" He winked at his woman who was busy with a bowl of batter preparing some johnny cakes.

Gabe frowned, looked toward the back wall of the cabin. They had put in a back wall to separate their living quarters from the massive cavern that opened behind the narrowing of the initial grotto. The large cavern was used as storage for the meat supply, keeping it cool but not freezing and well-protected. Although there was a back entrance they had enlarged to make it possible to take horses through, they had also blocked it off with brush and more to discourage any hibernating animals. The door to the dividing wall stood just away from the fireplace and Gabe sat up and looked toward the door. He lifted his hand to silence the others and listened.

He scowled and slowly rose, whispered back to Ezra, "Did you hear that?"

"Didn't hear anything," he answered in a whisper.

Gabe's hand dropped to the butt of his ever-present belt pistol, a .54 caliber, turn-over double-barreled pistol from the English craftsman, Joseph Bailes. He stepped toward the door, listening with every quiet step. Suddenly a scratch at the door caused him to stop, look back at Ezra to see if he heard it and saw his friend nod. He looked back at the door, heard something else he couldn't identify, frowned, and stepped nearer. He reached for the drop-bar, slowly lifted it and with cocked pistol in hand, flung open the door.

The door hit something, but it was small and not easily seen in the darkness. Gabe gave a quick search, saw nothing threatening, then looked down to see what the door hit. A ball of black fur wiggled at his feet with a tiny squeal, and in the darkness, Gabe saw two tiny eyes that seemed to glow blue, then white teeth bared in the midst of the black. He stepped back, looking at the little creature at his feet, looked around as far as he could see in the darkness, but nothing moved and no other sound than the little squeal at his feet. He reached down and scooped up the furball, recognizing it as a wolf pup, blacker than the darkness it came from, and wiggling in his grasp trying to free itself.

From behind came the question, "What is it?" from Ezra, anticipating an answer of some threatening danger and Gabe answered, "A wolf!"

"A wolf! Where? How'd it get in? Where is it?" The rapid-fire questions coming from all three of those behind him.

"It's a big one! Look out!" he shouted as he turned, holding the pup in his arms at his chest and grinning.

"Ohhhhh . . ." chorused the two women, coming closer and reaching out for the wiggly bundle of curiosity. Pale Otter took him from Gabe, holding it out and looking at its blue eyes, then turned to Gabe, "We need to find its mother!"

"Prob'ly in the cathedral!" declared Ezra, referring to the larger room of the cavern used to store their hanging meat and more. "Musta pushed her way through the brush at the back entry," he added.

"And if she's in there, she's probably gettin' into our meat!" declared Gabe, turning back to the now closed door. He looked back at Ezra, "Get your pistol and I'll light us a couple torches."

From their stack of sap covered branches just outside the door to the cavern, garnered from their many trips into the woods after poles for the cabin and trimming those poles, Gabe snatched up a pair, went to the fire and brought the torches to life. Handing one to Ezra, taking his pistol in hand, he led the way into the massive stalactite filled room they called the cathedral. The shadows danced among the limestone formations, bats hanging high above were undisturbed, and the cool air tugged at the tunics of the men.

Where the cavern narrowed, the tunnel walkway to the back entry beckoned. Gabe, careful with his steps on the wet slippery floor, held the torch high, pistol at the ready. Wolves were dangerous adversaries, and a mother protecting her young would be even more wary. But nothing stirred, no sound but the dripping of water from the icicle type stalactites, until Gabe stopped, lifted the torch high and spoke softly over his shoulder to Ezra, "There, on the ledge yonder," nodding to the slight widening of the walk toward a natural shelf that hung no more than two feet above the floor. Thick grey hair contrasted with the tawny color of the formations, but still nothing moved.

As they cautiously stepped nearer, Gabe saw sightless eyes above an open mouth with a dry tongue hanging to the side. Dried blood covered most of the wolf's neck and shoulders and part of her back. Lying at her protruding but flat nipples were two unmoving pups. All were dead. Gabe looked at Ezra, "She musta been attacked by somethin', maybe the rest of her pack, or a cougar, or . . ." he shrugged his shoulders, unknowing.

"We need to get 'em outta here, or buried, or somthin'. They'll start stinkin' once it warms up," declared Ezra.

"Yeah, but it'll wait till after breakfast," suggested Gabe, looking to his friend for confirmation.

Ezra chuckled, "You ain't never seen the day I'd pass up eatin' for work!"

2 / Scavenging

"Yes, most of this land, the Wind River Mountains and more, is the land of the Shoshone," answered Pale Otter as Gabe was questioning about the land, both near and far.

"And beyond the land of the Shoshone? Farther north, I mean," he asked. The two couples were seated at the table, each with a cup of steaming coffee/chicory before them. Gabe and Ezra had been talking earlier about their plans for spring, guessing it to be about the end of March, first of April, and hoping for an early spring in the mountains.

"Beyond the land of the Shoshone, is the land of the Apsáalooke, or the Crow. There is also the Blackfoot, the Gros Ventre and the Flathead."

"And are any of them friendly?" asked Gabe.

Otter lowered her head, looked at her cup, considering how to answer these questions of her man, a good man, but in many ways ignorant of the people native to these lands. "Any people can be both friendly and warlike. Some, like the Blackfoot, are feared by others because of the many raids they make, and some, like the Crow, can be both feared and friendly. The leader of a band or village might choose to be friendly if it is good for his people, but others do not want anyone in their land at any time."

"I think what she's tryin' to tell you is that any o' them natives we haven't met, are just like those we have. Depends on their leader and what's goin' on around 'em at the time," suggested Ezra. "Ain't no different where we come from. There's towns that are friendly and some that are plain mean all on account o' who's in control at the time."

"I s'pose you're right. I guess I was hopin' to find more that were usually friendly than not, but I reckon our journey out here is not just about meeting the native peoples. There's a lot of country to see and explore and there's somethin' else we need to consider, and that's supplies, if we want any."

"Want any?" asked an incredulous Ezra. "Want any? What about flour, sugar, cornmeal, and coffee! Not to mention gunpowder, lead, and such. Want any! But where we gonna get it?"

"Dunno. Course, there's always Santa Fe down south, but I was thinkin' we wanted to go north. Then the only thing north is a random French trader with

Hudson's Bay company or the Northwest Company, but I'm not too sure where they might have a tradin' post."

"We know there's one at Grand Forks on the Missouri. So, I'm thinkin' those Frenchies with the Hudson's Bay company have somethin' upstream o' there," suggested Ezra.

"Well, we could always do with what we got," surmised Gabe, grinning a little.

Ezra looked at him skeptically, "I know we can and have done without some things, but it's mighty hard to shoot a rifle without gunpowder and lead!"

"We can always make our own," drawled Gabe. He waited a moment then continued, "That white crystal looking stuff on the wall of the cave is saltpeter, and when we took the last elk last fall, I saw a band of yellow clay lookin' stuff that I think is sulfur. All we need to add is charcoal and I'm pretty sure we have plenty of that."

Ezra frowned, "You mean like we did when we were kids in the woods back east?"

"Exactly! And galena is pretty common, so I think we have everything we need for powder and shot."

A slow smile began to paint Ezra's face as he looked from Gabe to the women, "And with the villagers' corn crop, or as they call it, maize, we can have our corn meal for johnny cakes, and the way these ladies find everything else we need, we might be purty well set!"

Gabe chuckled as he stood, "So, with that to ease our minds, I think the horses would like to get some fresh graze. The way the warm sun's been melting the snow, I think that upper pasture might offer some for them." He led the way, trailing the big black Andalusian stallion, Ebony, followed by the little sorrel mare used as a packhorse. Ezra led his bay gelding and the steeldust mustang mare while Pale Otter led her blue roan gelding and the grulla mustang mare leaving Grey Dove to lead her buckskin gelding. With the large overhang of the granite monolith and the great maw that undercut, the men had used half of the opening for their cabin, but with a dividing wall down the middle, fashioned a stable for the horses' shelter. With their winter supply of grass depleted, the need for fresh graze weighed heavy upon them and the horses were excited about getting out of the stable into the fresh air and hopefully some fresh graze.

Gabe threw the lead rope over Ebony's neck, grabbed a handful of mane at his withers and swung himself aboard. He started to look back at the others but Ebony dropped his head between his knees and hunched his back as Gabe grabbed mane and tucked his heels behind the front legs of the stallion and pulled on the lead rope. But the stallion was anxious to stretch things out and planted his front feet and kicked at the clouds. "Whoa! Hold on there!" shouted

Gabe, tugging at the lead to lift the stallion's head. The big black lifted his head for a moment, dropped it again as he lunged forward, and with another high kick, launched Gabe over his head.

The deep snow drift at the edge of the long line of bushes in front of the cabin was a welcome sight as Gabe cartwheeled end over end to land in the cold white pillow. He scrambled to his feet, wiping snow from his face and neck and looked around with blazing eyes for his horse. Standing no more than ten feet away, the big black stretched out his neck, peeled his lips back from his teeth and gave Gabe an extended horse laugh. Gabe shook his head as he dusted the snow from his clothes, looked at the others who were trying to stifle their own laughter, then let a laugh escape from his own lips.

"You are the first flying bear I have ever seen!" declared a giggling Otter, putting a hand to her mouth to hide her laughter.

"Maybe we should change his name to Great White Stork! He has long legs and can fly like one!" declared a laughing Grey Dove.

Gabe glared at Ezra, "What do you have to say?" he growled.

Ezra chuckled, "Me? Far be it from me to make fun of my friend!" then turning to the women, "I'm thinkin' more of a duck!"

The women laughed again, and Gabe snatched

up the lead line of the black, who tossed his head as if he was agreeing with the others, and led the way, walking, to the upper pasture. As expected, the wide-open meadow was mostly free of snow, the only white being at the downhill end where drifts had blown up against the rocks and patches of white in the thicker trees where the sun failed to reach. There were tufts of brown grass left from the previous summer, and in a few places, early sprouts of green dared to show themselves as they stretched toward the faraway sun.

They stripped the ropes and riatas from the horses and let them run. They kicked their heels at the sky, twisted and ran, manes and tails flying, enjoying the fresh air and sunshine. Although there were many times during the winter months the horses had been taken out, ridden and grazed, each new time was a liberating moment for the animals. And they, like their people, were not immune to spring fever and often lifted their heads to the warm sunshine.

The men found a seat on a broad flat slab of granite and the women, at Otter's suggestion, went to the small stream at the bottom of the meadow where a shallow bog held cattails. They anticipated getting some of the fresh shoots, considered a delicacy, for their meals. As the men soaked up the sunshine and watched the horses, they were surprised by the whistle of a marmot. But when it was quickly repeated, Gabe recognized it as a call from Pale Otter, a signal she had used before. He elbowed Ezra as he slid from the rock, bringing his rifle from his back and starting toward the lower end of the meadow at a trot, watching the trees for any danger.

They spotted the women, standing together and looking at the ground at their feet. When the men appeared, the women motioned for silence but to hurry close. As they drew near, Otter dropped to one knee, pointing at the ground, while Dove watched the woods, motioning for Ezra to do the same as she whispered to him. Gabe dropped beside Otter, looked at where she pointed and his eyes flared, looked at Otter as she whispered, "Grizzly! Big boar! Fresh." She pointed to the sky, "One hand, less." Gabe knew she meant the tracks to be less than an hour old and the big bear could be nearby. He looked at the tracks again, reached out to place his spread hand in the middle and saw the track was wider by at least an inch on both sides of his extended hand, which measured over nine inches across.

He shook his head as he stood, gripping his rifle close to his chest and glancing down to ensure the cap was down underneath the half-cocked hammer. He looked at Ezra, mouthed the words, "Tracks almost a foot wide!"

Ezra's eyes flared and he glanced at the tracks and back at Gabe, shrugging his shoulders in a question as to what they should do.

Gabe answered softly, "We need to get the horses away!" He looked at the women, "Ezra and I will walk the tree line, you two go for the horses, but take it easy. If they smell that bear, no tellin' what they'll do."

The women nodded and started into the meadow. Gabe motioned for Ezra to follow as he started out, paralleling the tree line but staying about ten yards inside the meadow. The trees were not thick, a smattering of cedar, piñon, juniper and a few big ponderosa, and he could easily see into the woods. But he also knew any of the trees could hide the beast if he was stalking the horses.

The meadow was a little less than half a mile long and about two hundred yards wide of rolling flat. A small stream bed cut through the middle and carried spring runoff as it twisted its way through before dropping off the shoulder to make its way to the Popo Agie River. The morning breeze came from the north, blowing across the meadow toward the trees that held the bear. Gabe felt the wind, motioned to Ezra and nodded against the wind. Ezra nodded his understanding, keeping pace with Gabe. They stretched out to keep themselves between the horses and the trees, long strides that covered the distance quickly.

The women were nearing the horses, Dove

catching her buckskin and putting the rope around his neck before fashioning the nose loop for a halter, when Ebony lifted his head, ears up, nostrils flaring, and tossed his head. He reared up, pawing at the air, and whinnied at the other horses, doing his part as herd stallion. Gabe saw the actions of Ebony, turned back to Ezra, "He smells the bear!" and started at a run along the tree line, searching the trees for any movement. He glanced at Ebony, saw the big black herding the other horses away from the trees in the general direction of the cabin, and looked to the trees. Movement! It was big, brown, and moving fast!

The massive grizzly burst from the trees and lumbered toward the horses. Ebony spun around, reared up, and screamed a challenge to the big bruin. The bear stopped, startled, then rose up on his hind legs, head cocked to the side, and let loose a timber rattling roar. His mouth stretched wide, long teeth showing, tongue lolling, and huge paws clawing at the air as he answered the challenge of the herd stallion.

Gabe was almost two hundred yards from the scene and was frantically running, determined to stop any fight, knowing that even if Ebony were to defeat the grizzly, there was no way he could not be injured or even killed. Gabe grabbed at his belt pistol, and without missing a stride, he brought it up, bringing it to full cock and aimed it high over the bear, and fired. The blast spat smoke and lead, but Gabe didn't expect it to do any damage, just distract the beast. He jammed the pistol back in his belt, brought the hammer of his Ferguson rifle to full cock, all while he continued running. Then when he saw the bear drop to all fours and look his direction, he dropped to one knee, brought up the rifle and took aim at the top predator of the Rockies.

The bear stared, unmoving, looking at this new threat. Gabe was on one knee, Ezra just dropping to his knee to bring his rifle to his shoulder, and the big beast cocked his head to the side, split his face and let out another roar that reverberated across the meadow, echoing from the granite sided mountain, letting every living thing know he was the biggest beast in the mountains. With a glance at the horses, the big grizzly turned away and casually strolled back into the trees.

Gabe let out a big breath, looked at Ezra and back at the trees as he slowly stood. Both men looked at the horses and the women, who were busy gathering the skittish horses together. Both men shook their heads, lowered their rifles to their side as they gently lowered the hammers, and with another lingering stare at the trees, started for the women.

3 / Renegades

"We been all the way to the Pacific with MacKenzie and all over this country with Thompson. We traded with the Chippewa, the Dene, and Indians I can't even pronounce. We worked with Hudson's Bay and North West and look at us, we ain't got nothin' to show for it all!" declared Jacques Beauchamp. He kicked at the hot coals, stirred them with a stick and sat back, still staring into the flames of the campfire. Across the glow that split the dark night, the fire shone on the bearded face of Charles Ducette and three other men, all attired in the fashion of the coureur de bois. Buckskin breeches with high-topped lace up boots, woolen shirts open at the neck to show the red wool union suit long underwear. Two had knit caps pulled down to their ears, one had a floppy felt hat that shaded his dark eyes and Ducette sat rubbing his hands through his long curly hair that hung shoulder length.

Peter Marchand, Raphael Moreau, and Rene Morgan had joined the camp of the two men earlier in the evening. With the common ground of history with either Hudson's Bay or North West company, the three men had no argument with the voiced complaints of Beauchamp. Although younger than the two men at the camp, they were just as disgruntled with the changes that had happened since the recent signing of the Jay Treaty. Although Marchand was a Métis, his loyalty and that of his friends had always been with the French, but with the treaty, the French were no longer in power, nor were the British and even the boundary between the United States and Rupert's Land was ambiguous.

"So, how's a man s'posed to make a living?" questioned Marchand.

Beauchamp kicked at the coals again, snatched a piece of fresh venison that dripped juices into the flames from the willow branch that held it and more. He took a bite of the hot but rare meat and chewed for a moment as he thought. He lifted his eyes to the younger man that asked the question, judging him to be in his late twenties or maybe early thirties, then growled, "I been studyin' on that a spell. There's still a market for furs, long's we don't hafta take what Hudson pays, which ain't much. If we can get us a good bunch o' furs, take 'em downriver to trade 'em with the 'mericans, I think we could do alright fer ourselves."

"Downriver? Where?" asked Moreau.

"Depends on where we start. The Missouri dumps into the Mississippi at that new town called Saint Louis. Then anywhere 'tween there an' New Orleans, or even there if'n we wanna. I figger that any place to the south will offer better prices than Hudson's!"

"Ain't never been to New Orleans. Wanted to, though," mumbled Morgan as he looked at Moreau and nodded.

"But, where we get the money to buy supplies to trade with the Indians?" asked Marchand.

"Trade? Ain't plannin' on tradin'. Figger we just take what we want. We can take supplies from any o' the tradin' posts that are out in the middle o' nowhere, and we can take the furs from the Indians whenever we want. They ain't got no guns, leastways most of 'em don't," explained Beauchamp, grunting and chewing between comments. He wiped his greasy hands on the buckskin breeches, belched and grabbed a jug of rum and tipped it with his elbow to take a long draught.

"But, there's only five of us here. What can we do against some o' them Indian villages that have a hundred or more warriors?" inquired Morgan.

Beauchamp belched again, set the jug down, and looked at the man asking the question. He was a

slender man, tall and lanky, light complexion and
stringy brown hair that trailed over his ears from
under the woolen cap that held the rebellious hair
under cover. About the same age as the other, his
furtive glances and nervous manner didn't sit well
with the older man. But he answered, "Only five,
now. I know there's plenty others feel the same, an'
there's lots o' renegade Indians that'll do anything
for some o' this," he declared, patting the crock of
rum.

"I dunno. I'd hafta give that some thought,"
declared Marchand.

The language of the five, though in English when
their native tongue was French, had become over
the years, the language of trade. With the British in
control of most of the forts, and many of the tribes
learning that language, their common tongue had
become the conglomeration of needful slang and
descriptive language of trade. Their conversation
continued into the night until one by one they
turned into their blankets, but with no place to go the
following day, most slept late, their snores, coughs,
and belches adding nothing to the harmonies of the
night.

The three newcomers had drawn off by themselves
to discuss the proposition of the older and more
experienced coureur de bois. Men that had spent at
least a decade longer dealing with the many tribes

and traveling the wilderness to arrange and make trades for the valuable furs taken by the natives. But it's one thing to work for others and eke out a living when they take advantage of you, and quite another to cross the line and go against everything you've been taught and taken as your standard of character or moral boundaries. And what was the alternative? To continue to slave away letting others take advantage of your sacrifices or turn the tables and become the one who takes what they need and want and perhaps build your own fortune and one day retire from this life of depredation and misery.

"So, what do you think?" asked Marchand as he looked at his two friends, men he had partnered with and toiled with for the last two seasons.

Raphael Moreau was the first to reply, "What choice do we have? To stay with the company and have a life with no place to lay our head but under the trees in the wilderness and nothing to eat but what we kill, and taking enough to buy supplies for another season, or . . .?" He shrugged as he glanced from Marchand to Morgan.

Morgan dropped his eyes, lifted his foot to rest on a downed log, leaned his elbow on his knee as he looked at his friends. "I've always been honest, never took anything that didn't belong to me, worked hard at whatever I done, and prided myself on bein' a good man. But like he said, what do we have to show for it? Maybe we can go along with 'em for a spell, see what happens, an' if we don't like it, we can always leave. Won't be any the worse off than we are right now."

Moreau and Marchand stared at Morgan, then looked at one another. Marchand shrugged and sat down on the log as he looked from one to the other then answered, "I think you're right. We've got to do something cuz we're almost out of supplies, so, it's either commit to the company or leave, and I'd just as soon try it on our own. I've known a few other coureur de bois that have done alright. The other choice is to get a permit and become a voyageur but all that does is give us a little bigger cut of the take, but I ain't seen any o' them doin' all that well."

"I heard from one o' the trappers at the rendezvous at Grand Portage that the price of furs anyplace but Hudson's was at least twice what they were payin'," added Moreau.

"There's always been talk like that but I ain't seen very many takin' off on their own to go after those higher prices," commented Marchand.

"It's like Beauchamp said, if you don't have the money for the trade goods and the traps for beaver, what are you gonna do but take what either company offers. They got us over a barrel, and they know it," spat Morgan, tossing a stick into the trees in disgust.

"This is a big step my friends. We'll be stealin'

from the posts, raiding and stealing from the natives, and on the run from both," suggested Marchand.

"Well, the way I see it, the companies have been stealin' from us, so we'll just be takin' back what's rightly ours," replied Morgan.

The other two nodded their heads in agreement, but none were anxious to take their decision to Beauchamp. Once that was done, there didn't seem to be any turning back, although they had convinced themselves they could leave at any time. But once that line has been crossed, can one ever turn back?

4 / Spring

"Ow! His teeth are sharp!" exclaimed Gabe. The wolf pup had grown considerably in the past couple weeks, his blue eyes now blazed a golden orange, his downy fur had turned to a deep pile, his paws were almost as big as Gabe's palms, and his spunk had increased almost daily. He had taken to Otter more than any of the others, but he was playful with them all and sometimes his playfulness portrayed and foretold of his true heritage as a pack leader. Otter guessed him to be about two to three moons which Gabe interpreted as about ten to twelve weeks, but he guessed the pup to be a bit older. He stood mid-calf high to Gabe and he could eat as much as Ezra. But he had brought a new liveliness to the cabin that had sometimes become a bit confining for everyone.

Gabe and Otter lay on the floor before the fireplace, facing one another, with the pup between them. The wolf lay on his side, his back against Otter's belly and facing Gabe. "He looks like he's protecting you!" declared Gabe, a little jealousy showing in his tone and expression.

"He is. That's what a pack leader does, he protects those of his pack against all others."

"Well, aren't we all a part of the same pack?" asked Gabe, reaching toward the wolf who snapped at his hand that Gabe quickly withdrew.

"Yes. He just likes some of us better than others." Otter chuckled, then added, "Maybe he sees you as a threat."

"IIe's the only threat around here!" answered Gabe, rolling to his back but still looking at Otter as she played with the pup.

Gray Dove sat at the table with Ezra watching the pair on the floor and began, "The wolf is important to our people. Some see him as the creator god with great power. He has been the totem of Otter since she was very young. His little brother, the coyote, is known as a trickster and the story is told how he tried to trick Wolf, who has the power to bring life back to those who have crossed over. Coyote tried to stop the power of Wolf when he said he should not bring anyone back to life because there would be no room for everyone. Coyote hoped this would make our people hate him, but Wolf turned the trick on Coyote when Coyote's son died, and Wolf did not bring him back. Our people say that is how death came to our people and our lands, and that is why we weep when a loved one crosses over. But Wolf has great power and wisdom and is important to our people."

Gabe looked at the playful pup then to Otter, "What do your people think about you having a wolf in our lodge?"

"They know the wolf will do as he pleases and if he chooses to stay in our lodge, that is a sign of power," she answered, stroking the wolf's head and shoulders as he stretched under her attention.

"Hmmm, interesting. He might be a good addition to the clan," replied Gabe, glancing at Ezra and Dove who sat smiling and watching.

"So, what'cha gonna call him?" asked Ezra, looking at Otter.

Otter frowned, a question written on her expression as she asked, "Call him?"

"Yeah, you know. A name, like I'm Ezra, she's Grey Dove, you know."

"Wolf. That what he is and that's what he is called, Wolf."

Ezra chuckled, pursed his lips as he looked at Gabe who was grinning. Gabe shrugged and kept his peace. He knew it would be useless to try to argue or explain and there was nothing wrong with calling the little furball Wolf, so, he saw no reason to change things. He sat up, put his arms around his knees and looked at the others, "So, spring is here and I'm gettin' restless. What say we head up north and have a look at this wild country. From what Otter says, there's a lot of mountains and mysteries that she hasn't seen but has heard stories about and this might be a good time to make some new discoveries."

Ezra grinned, "That's what I've been waitin' to hear. Every time we climb this rock and have our morning time with the Lord, I can't help but look to the mountains and to the north and wonder what's waiting for us." He looked over at Grey Dove who had reached out for his hand and squeezed it as she smiled broadly.

"Then, maybe we should get to packin' and get ready. Time's a wastin'!" answered Gabe as he stood to his feet. He looked at Dove and back at Otter, both had dropped their eyes and sat still, not looking at their men. He asked Otter, "What's wrong?"

Otter stood, still looking at the floor and spoke quietly, "What do you want me to pack for you?"

Gabe glanced at Dove who still sat quiet, eyes down, then to Ezra who was frowning and looking at Gabe. The men were a little concerned at the manner of the women and didn't immediately understand. Gabe looked at Otter again, "Well, I think we'll just take the two mustangs for pack animals, they should be able to carry everything we need, what with the parfleches with pemmican and other food stuff. We'll carry our own bedrolls and personal gear on our own horses. So, really it shouldn't take much packing to be ready."

Otter, still looking down, spoke quietly as she asked, "Do you want to take the big pot or leave it with us?"

Gabe frowned, looked at Ezra again who was looking at Dove with a frown. Gabe asked, "What do you mean, leave it? Won't you need it on the trail?"

Otter looked up at him, eyes wide, "You mean we will go too?"

Gabe chuckled, "Of course you'll go!" He looked at Dove, "Both of you will go! We're not about to leave you behind! Is that what you were thinking that gave you such a long face?"

Otter jumped and threw her arms around his neck and kissed him full on the lips, holding him as tight as she could, then drew back, tears in her eyes and a big smile on her face. "We thought you were going without us!" she declared, bouncing on her toes as she spoke. Gabe glanced over to see Dove hanging on Ezra in a similar fashion.

"Look, when we got married, or joined as your people call it, I told your father it was forever, and we would always be together. Wherever I go, you go!" Gabe looked to Ezra and added, "Didn't Ruth say something like that, ". . . whither thou goest, I will go; and where thou lodgest, I will lodge: thy people shall be my people, and thy God my God."

Otter looked at Gabe, a slight frown creasing her forehead, and asked, "Who is Ruth?"

Gabe chuckled, "A woman in the Bible. You know, the book that tells about our God."

Otter smiled, "I like what she says. Now, I must learn about your God."

Gabe smiled, glanced at Ezra and back at Otter, "You will, you will."

They rode into the rising sun as they followed the Popo Agie through the canyon and into the flats where the Wind River valley lay before them. Six horses, four riders, with one carrying a wolf pup on her lap. Although she had introduced the pup to the horses by taking him into the stable with her and letting each horse sniff and look him over, when they started off with the pup on her lap, the blue roan mare was a little skittish but settled down soon enough. Gabe was in the lead and stood in his stirrups as the rising sun bent its rays into the canyon and painted his face with the golden brilliance and warmth. He twisted around to smile at Otter who was watching the antics of her man and smiling, "It's a great day in the mountains!" he declared, almost shouting and hearing his words echo between the granite walls.

As they crossed the creek for the last time and broke into the open spaces of the valley, Gabe reined up and let the others come alongside. They were still high enough on the sloping shoulder of the mountain range that they could overlook the wide valley and the shadow of smaller mountains in the distance. The green in the valley bottom glistened and made Gabe think of his visit to Ireland and the dew on the moors at daybreak, but this land was more vast and unending. The Wind River and its tributaries carved their way through the rolling flats, sharing the wealth of water with the many meadows and plains.

Several deer had jumped from the willows by the creek and bounded away toward the valley bottom. A small herd of pronghorn grazed in the distance, always wary of any threat with half grazing and the rest watching. Splotches of color marked patches of early blooming flowers, with a patch of white and purple pasqueflower blossoms standing at attention on the hairy stems at their feet. A little further on they found a cluster of white lilies with faces open to the sun. Off their lower shoulder rose a wide patch of golden pea standing tall with multiple blooms on each stem. It was a beautiful day to start a memorable journey into the unexplored wilderness.

5 / Stone Stories

Once free of the canyon of the Popo Agie, the small party turned northwest to follow the greenery of spring. Shouldered by red clay rimrock on angled tablelands, the green valley lifted the spirits of those long entombed by winter's white blanket. They had gone less than three or four miles when Otter pointed, motioned to Dove, and the two gigged their horses to a trot toward a wide patch of lavender blossoms. They quickly reined up and slid from their horses and started pulling up several of the blossoming plants, giggling all the while. As Gabe and Ezra arrived, they looked at the women as if they had lost their minds, but Otter, seeing their consternation, laughed and said, "Timpsila!" pointing at the handful of pulled plants lying at her feet.

Ezra grinned, looked at Gabe, "That's what them Omaha called 'em, ain't it?"

Gabe chuckled, "Somethin' like that. They made for some good eating."

Otter started peeling the dark brown husk from the bulbous root of the plant as she walked to Gabe. She took a bite, then lifted the clean white globe to Gabe who took most of the remainder in one bite and began chewing the fresh, moist, root that reminded him of the meat of an apple. He grinned as he chewed and savored the flavor, watching Ezra do the same with the tidbit offered by Dove.

The women's bounty was added to the parfleche on the steeldust mustang and their journey continued in the shadow of the towering Wind River range. Both men marveled at the terrain, with the ridges rising on their right showing a rosy orange color that displayed itself below the rimrock. But the formations were what they thought were amazing. It appeared as if in eons past, this land was totally flat until something brought a cataclysmic disruption and split the earth in jagged lines, tilting up the break to stand as the upturned edge of flat tablelands. To their left, they were on the downhill side of a similar upheaval leaving the faraway ridges pointing upwards to the granite tipped peaks of the mountains.

The tallest butte had a long finger ridge that pointed into the narrow valley as if to separate the narrow creek-bottomed valley from the further red clay and ravine clawed land beyond. When they came upon a wide ravine with a creek in the bottom that crashed and splattered its way from the mountains, carrying the spring melt from the high country, they chose to follow it into the lowlands. With ample grasses on both sides, willows that bent low over the water, they chose to take a mid-day break and have some coffee and smoked meat with the new crop of prairie turnips.

They found some shade beneath a couple of gnarly cottonwoods and let the animals graze at their leisure. The women had prepared a small fire and had the timpsila baking in the coals, the meat hanging over the small flames, and the coffeepot dancing at the side. Gabe was reclined against a small log and was idly looking at the butte that lay above them. With two rows of rimrock that stood in contrast to the dull red of the soil between them, Gabe shaded his eyes when something looked amiss at the flat face of the higher rock. He sat up, frowning and through squinted eyes, stared at the upper wall.

He walked to his saddle and retrieved his telescope from the saddlebags and returned to his place near the log. He lifted the glass to his eye and focused in on the object of interest, scowled, lowered the glass and shook his head. He brought the glass up again, held it steady and slowly examined the image as best he could from afar. When he lowered the scope again, he noticed the others were watching him and he let a slow grin paint his face. "I was looking at that upper cliff face. There appears to be something carved up there. I'd like to go take a closer look."

"May I see?" asked Otter, coming closer.

"Sure," answered Gabe, handing the scope to her as he began to explain how to use the optical instrument. She lifted it to her eye, drew back suddenly and looked at Gabe, then lifted it again and did as he instructed to focus it to clarity. She held the glass steady and said, "Those are stories in stone. They are found in many places. People of old would tell their stories there and many still do."

"Petroglyphs," said Gabe. "Those stories in stone are seen all over the world. We'll go up there after we eat," he suggested, looking at the others. The rest of the group smiled, and nodded, as they turned to the fire for their mid-day meal.

Shortly after starting their ascent, they crossed an ancient game trail that appeared to make its way to the top and Gabe started after. It crisscrossed the face of the slope, turned into a notch that cut through the first line of rimrock and twisted its way to the shelf that held the flat cliff face with the markings. When they neared, Gabe stopped and surveyed the panoramic cliff canvas used by ancient artisans to say they were here.

"You said these were stories in stone, can you tell what they say?" asked Gabe, looking to Pale Otter who was focused on the images before her.

She turned to Gabe, smiled and nodded, then pointed to a cluster of images high above them. "That tells of a good year. The first image is the shaman, with the buffalo headdress, the next is of a chief with the hair bone chest plate, that is the thunderbird that watches over the people. That image," pointing at a larger image in the middle of the group, "is women making pemmican and that one is showing a time of plenty with meat on a drying rack. You can see it is a woman with her tunic holding the decoration of elk's teeth and quills."

"So, what you're saying is the Shaman told the chief it would be a good year because the thunderbird is watching. And because of the images of pemmican and drying meat, that shows it was a good year," said Gabe, looking at his woman.

"Yes, and that is an elk herd, and a buffalo herd, and those are the hunters," she explained pointing out the figures obviously on horseback with bows and arrows chasing the herds. "It was a good year, but that group shows different." She moved closer, frowning and looking at the lower images, "This is a very different story. See the clouds? There were bad storms in winter, but no rain in summer. They moved camp but only had fish and some antelope for food. They did a dance, but no rain came, and many died." The images were easily seen and understood once she explained the story. Others were not grouped and seemed to be simpler stories such as one that showed a canoe with warriors but nothing else. Others were not as easily distinguished but the entire cliff face was a story in itself that told of people of generations past that had the same need to be remembered and stories told as that of all people around the world.

They turned back to the northwest, crossed a small river that Dove said was the Little Wind River, and took a trail that followed a small feeder creek that cut its way between two distant up thrusts of land. While that off their right shoulder stretched about a mile and a half to the crest of a series of yellow mounds that stood about three hundred feet higher than the valley floor and formed the north boundary, that off their left shoulder was more than two miles distant, but rose about twice as high and had the appearance of a saw-tooth range with a jagged line of white that appeared at the base of the ragged ridge. Gabe had noticed the far side of that ridge when they came from the place of the petroglyphs and had thought it to be a line of mounds, streaked by the Creator's brush with lines of varied shades and widths. The valley they followed ended in a wide basin that held the headwaters of the small creek that had its origin with several springs that were cradled in a cluster of cottonwoods and willows.

After letting the horses refresh themselves in the cool spring water, Gabe pointed Ebony to the low rising rim of the basin and goaded him up the clay slope. They quickly mounted the ridge to see the valley of the Wind River about five miles distant. He looked at the sun, gauged the time, and pushed on to the river. They had previously decided to follow the river to its headwaters and then decide to either cross over the Wind River range or to turn to the east into Crow country.

As they crested a butte overlooking the winding Wind River, they sat their horses and enjoyed the panoramic view of the flats and the river valley. From their promontory, they could see a turquoise colored gem of a lake lying in the midst of a wide green basin. About five miles off, it was easy to see this lake would be a magnet for wildlife of the area. With dry land that held little else but sagebrush, grease wood, and cacti, the jewel of water shone bright in spite of the setting sun behind them. Gabe looked at Otter, "Kinda purty, huh?"

"Yes. My people have come here before when the buffalo come to the valley early. But that is also a place for the Crow and Cheyenne." She nodded toward the lake, "There is smoke from a large camp now."

Gabe looked again, and with the sun at their back, the whispery grey of smoke slowly lifted from the valley floor. "I see. Looks like it might be a sizable village, too."

"It is best we do not go there. If it is Crow or Cheyenne, we would have to fight."

"But, could it be another band of Shoshone?" asked Gabe.

"No, I do not think so. My people stay in the mountains, come only to hunt buffalo. The herds are not here, it is too early. These hunt antelope, deer, fish, and elk. They might stay until the buffalo come, but sometimes they do not."

Gabe stood in his stirrups, looking over the twisting Wind River, pointed out a wide bend that showed a lot of green, "That looks like a likely place to camp."

Otter looked where he pointed, then glanced back at her man. "See where the green is? That is the riverbed where floodwaters cover. The river is fast and muddy." She nodded to the north west, "The sun had been warm on the mountains and the water will rise, perhaps tonight it will flood that place. But if we go there," she pointed to a shoulder with scattered piñon and juniper, "we can take our horses to water, but sleep where it is dry."

Gabe dropped his eyes, shook his head slightly, and without another word, pushed Ebony toward the edge of the butte and started toward the place chosen by Otter. It had been their practice to find graze and water close by, but if what Otter said was right, and he had no reason to believe otherwise, water would not be their friend on this night.

6 / Flood

Ebony jerked his head up and let a low rumble come from deep within, a sound of warning that even the sleeping Gabe recognized. He came awake instantly but moved only his eyes as he looked at the big black standing head up, ears pointing and wide eyes staring down the slope to something that had alarmed him in the valley bottom. Gabe heard the ruckus before he saw it, the crashing, rumbling and splashing of floodwaters just as Otter had predicted. He rose from his blankets and in the dim light of the moon and stars, looked below to see the wall of water push over the low bank of the grassy flat, moving everything in its path as it carried its own cargo of brush, logs, and more. Piñon and juniper bent before the onslaught, some overwhelmed and buried beneath the muddy waters. Within seconds, the entire peninsula that pushed into the bend of the river was submerged, nothing showing but the debris carried by the overflow.

"It is as I said," came the voice from slightly behind and beside him. Otter reached her hand through his crooked elbow and drew near. "It will be like that for days. Perhaps not as strong but still deep. There is much snow in the high mountains and warm weather brings it down quickly."

"And as you said, if we had camped there we would have lost everything. There would not have been time to get away." He looked down at her upturned face, "If you hadn't been with us . . ." he shook his head at the thought.

"What's all the racket?" asked Ezra, still in his blankets but sitting up. He knew if there was any danger, Gabe would have his rifle and wouldn't just be standing there in the moonlight with his arm around Otter.

"Flood, just like Otter said," answered Gabe. "Go back to sleep. We got a few more hours 'fore first light."

The only answer that came from Ezra was a groan as he lay back next to Grey Dove. Gabe chuckled at his friend, looked down at Otter, "Maybe we should get a little more shut-eye while we can, ya' reckon?"

The remainder of the night, Gabe was restless as he listened to the continual sounds of the flood below. His thoughts wandered from reminiscences of his

youth in the woods with Ezra to the events of the
duel and the beginning of their long journey. It had
been a couple of years since they left Philadelphia,
and those years had been a continual adventure,
more than they had anticipated or even dreamed
about in their many jaunts in the woods as young
men. The year they left was full of major events that
would shape or change the future of their world.
Things such as the Jay Treaty which came after the
Treaty of Paris that ended the Revolutionary War
and changed the face of the vast wilderness west of
the Mississippi. Although it was prompted partially
by the French Revolutionary Wars, it resolved issues
between the British and America. With Britain and
France at war, things were changing in America,
specifically the control of the western wilderness
known as Spanish Louisiana. Because of the war
with Britain, France had surrendered control of the
wilderness to the Spanish, but that was a tenuous
hold at best.

It was that very wilderness that Gabe and Ezra
now occupied and were exploring. Gabe had long
thought this land would eventually become a part
of the United States and he and Ezra wanted to be
among the first Americans to explore this land. But
one of the problems with controlling governments
that held lands they did not know was they
overlooked the current residents of this vast land,

and Gabe knew the controlling nation must make peace with the many tribes if there was to ever be an expansion of the nation into this country.

He rolled over in his blankets, lifted his eyes to the moon and guessed there remained about an hour before first light. He crawled out from under the heavy blankets, picked up his rifle and Bible and started up the bluff to spend some time with his Lord and greet the day. It was an easy climb, watching his step around the patches of prickly pear cactus and twisting his way through the cholla, but he soon crested the butte and found a seat on a slab of sandstone. He turned to the east and used the light of the moon to barely make out the words of Psalm 91, He shall cover thee with his feathers, and under his wings shalt thou trust: his truth shall be thy shield and buckler. Thou shalt not be afraid for the terror by night; nor for the arrow that flieth by day. He smiled at the thought of the terror of the night when the flood came crashing through and he could only imagine what the arrow by day would mean, but he knew his God was in control of all things and he was willing to put his trust in Him completely.

The eastern sky was beginning to show grey before the Creator began to paint the empty canvas with the usual colors of morning. The underbellies of several clouds were blushing pink and Gabe dropped his gaze to the far bank of the river. Movement had caught his eye and he scanned the bank with its intermittent timber and brush, watching, waiting, knowing the peripheral vision would be more apt to catch sight of any movement than his direct stare and he continued his scan. Then there was movement at a break in the trees, two, three, no, five men were gathered, apparently to watch the cascade of the floodwaters, perhaps to see if it would be crossable. Gabe saw one of the men turn and trot toward the encampment that lay beyond a low ridge near the lake he spotted yesterday. He looked below at their camp, then across the river to the bank where the men stood. Realizing they could and had probably already seen their camp, he snatched up his rifle and Bible and started back to the camp.

His long strides and slides soon took him down the slope to find the women busy at the cookfire. Ezra came trotting into camp right after, and Gabe said, "We got comp'ny!"

"I saw 'em. Five of 'em, but they were afoot. I think they were surprised to see our camp," replied Ezra, reaching for a warmed up johnny cake.

"One of 'em took off toward their camp, prob'ly to tell the others. We'll know soon e'nuff. I don't think they'll try to cross the river, but I think we need to start packin' up anyway. No sense in hangin' around here." He also picked up a johnny cake, snatched a strip of sizzling meat from a willow withe and started for the packs and saddles.

Their camp was in the scattered piñon and juniper, but not well protected. The river below, was usually about sixty or seventy yards wide, but with the floodwaters, it spanned about a hundred yards. Just below their camp, the river turned back toward the butte, pushed up against a wall of rock that stood about seventy feet above the water, and made its way downstream, rushing all the while. The warriors from the encampment, presumed to be Crow, had returned with several other mounted warriors. Gabe watched as the group talked, gesticulating toward the camp of the two men and two women, and argued among themselves. Finally two men stepped to the water's edge, lifted their bows and sent arrows across the stream with a high arc, but the arrows fell from that arc to impale themselves at the foot of a line of willows that hung long branches into the rushing water. The bowmen turned to the others, waving their arms and shouting, obviously explaining that no one could shoot an arrow across.

Two of the mounted warriors hollered, then gigged their horses toward the water and started to cross, but the lead horse reared up and dropped his rider into the water when he turned and headed back to the shore, the second horse also turned away from the strong current and staggered back to the bank. The unseated rider fought the water and Gabe saw the man crawl from the river more than a hundred yards downstream.

Gabe looked at Ezra, "You watchin' this?"

Ezra chuckled, "Yeah. It's almost funny. And if they weren't tryin' to get across so they could lift our scalps, I'd think it was funny."

"I hate to waste an arrow, but maybe I should give 'em a warning, what say?"

Ezra chuckled again, "Use one of your whistlers!"

Gabe retrieved the case with the Mongol bow and began to string the recurve weapon. It wasn't an easy task and Gabe had found the best way was to use his feet near the grip and with both hands bring the risers back to nock the string. He stood and slipped one of the whistling arrows from his quiver. The arrows held a hollowed piece of bone on the shaft just behind the arrowhead that made the unique sound in flight. Gabe stepped into the clearing, grabbed his jacket and waved it overhead to get the attention of the Crow warriors. When he saw them stop and stare, he nocked the arrow, brought the bow to full draw and let the arrow fly.

From their camp to the place where the warriors were standing was about two hundred yards. An easy distance for the Mongol bow that Gabe had often used to send arrows twice that distance. His aim arced the arrow high overhead and the warriors watched, but when it came nearer and they could hear

the screaming high-pitched whistle over the sound
of the floodwaters, their reaction was obvious. They
looked at the arrow, glancing quickly to one another
and nervously moved about. The arrow flew high
over their heads and spiked itself in the dirt beside
a clump of greasewood beyond. Several warriors ran
to find the arrow and when the first man retrieved it,
he looked at it, held it high for the others to see and
went to the riverbank to see the man that did such a
feat.

They had finished gearing up the horses and were
ready to leave when Gabe watched the warriors
across the river. He mounted up, turned toward
the warriors and waved his hat in the air, watched
as they returned the wave, and the four moved out,
returning to the trail that followed the Wind River
toward its headwaters and into the Valley of the
Wind.

7 / Medicine Butte

The two couples rode about fifty yards off the west bank of the Wind River, following its twisted course as it carried the spring runoff from the high mountains. The cloudless, azure sky arched overhead as a canopy of protection for the travelers. The early summer sun had warmed them on their journey and aided the women in their continual search for tubers, roots, and blossoms that could be used as food or medicine. While the women watched the ground, the men kept their eyes on the trail and surrounding countryside. Always alert for any danger, they appreciated seeing the fingerprints of the Creator everywhere they looked. First it was a family of mule deer with spotted fawns scampering after their mothers, then a black bear with a pair of cubs, and then a small herd of elk or wapiti with young bulls just sprouting stubby antlers and cows nudging the orange shaded calves ahead of the grazing herd.

When they stopped for a mid-day break, Gabe mounted a knob of a hill with scope in hand, showing a little concern of a possible pursuit by the Crow. But there was no one on their back trail and no sign of any danger in any direction. He watched the herd of elk climb a shoulder of a butte, finding new green sprouts of grass and flowers for their graze. A golden eagle glided with wide spread wings as he searched below for his dinner. Game was plentiful and showed little concern for the visitors to their territory which spoke of little hunting pressure and also told of the absence of any large band of natives camped nearby. He looked below at the makeshift camp and saw Otter standing, wolf pup at her feet, one hand on her hip, the other shading her eyes as she looked for her man. Gabe stood, waved and started down the slope to the camp.

He was greeted first by the pup nipping at his heels, then with a broad smile from Otter. He walked into her waiting arms, embraced her as he kicked at the sharp toothed pup, then turned to look at the black furball, "He's growin' mighty fast. He keeps that up, he'll be drawin' blood when he nips."

"He is learning from the pack leader," declared Otter, grinning at her man. "In a pack, the pups will play with the leader to learn about taking game. The leader also disciplines the pups with a bite or more."

"So, now I'm supposed to bite him?" asked Gabe, grinning at the mental image.

Otter giggled, "I would like to see that!"

Gabe pushed the pup away with his foot, "Then let's bite into some food. I'm hungry!"

***

As the sun sought sanctuary behind the western mountains, the travelers made camp on a shoulder of a small butte overlooking the wide river bottom. Below their camp a small feeder creek chuckled beneath overhanging willows searching for the deeper waters of the Wind River. The valley bottom was lush with greenery, grasses, choke cherry and service berry bushes, willows and random alder and cottonwood.

Once the stock was tended and picketed, Gabe and Ezra offered to go after fresh meat, anticipating deer or antelope coming for their evening drink. Gabe was seated on a log and using his feet to string his bow while Ezra checked the loads in his rifle and pistol, when Otter suggested, "If you see a turkey, it would be a good change. I would say get some fish, but the water is too muddy and high."

Gabe grinned, "If a gobbler makes himself known, we'll bring him back. But you'll have to pluck him!"

"You get him and gut him, and I will pluck him

and cook him!" she countered, grinning.

"Sounds like a deal!" answered Gabe as he stood, bow in hand and quiver hanging at his side. He looked to Ezra, nodded for him to lead the way and they started for the river bottom. Gabe pointed across the river to the flats beyond, "That flat topped butte yonder, Otter says it's a place of great medicine. She said some of the young warriors go up on top o' that butte when they go on their vision quest." The tall butte stood like a solitary sentinel overlooking the flats to the south and more. It was an impressive and unique sight, standing alone and almost a thousand feet higher than the river valley, with smaller knobs of hills huddled at its feet.

"I don't think I'd like to climb it. It looks almost straight up and down, 'cept for the rimrock at the top. Course I reckon you could almost see forever from up on top," commented Ezra, picking his way through the cacti and sage toward the river bottom.

They had gone less than two hundred yards when Ezra stopped in a slight crouch, frozen still, then signaled to Gabe to come near. "You hear that?" he whispered, pointing toward a cluster of scrub oak brush at the edge between the river and the bluff. The squawk, squawk, followed by a rolling gobble came from the edge of the brush as they watched three turkeys slowly walk into the clear, continually dropping their beaks to pick some tidbit from the ground before them.

The men were partially shielded from sight by a bunch of rabbit brush and Gabe stepped forward as he brought an arrow to draw. He chose the lead tom turkey and let the arrow fly. In a flutter of feathers, a loud squawk, and the other two turkeys taking awkward flight and run, the big tom went to ground, a single wing flapping once, twice, then it was still. Gabe retrieved the bird, quickly opened it up to gut it, then lay it atop a thick greasewood bush to pick up on their way back to camp. Then with a nod to Ezra, the two dropped off the edge of the bluff and into the green of the valley bottom.

In a short while, the men were hunched over the carcass of a young spike buck mule deer, field dressing it to ready it to take back to camp. The dim light of dusk offered ample light for their duties as they busied themselves, each to his own duty. Gabe had just pulled the pile of guts from the belly when he heard something that caught his attention. He stood, bloody hands at his side and looked up the draw on the opposite bank that carried a feeder stream into the Wind River. From somewhere in that draw came the unmistakable howl of a wolf, probably baying at the rising moon, crying for a partner or mate. But when an answering howl came from upstream on the river, Gabe glanced at Ezra, "You reckon that's a pack smellin' the blood?"

"Could be. Maybe the gut pile will keep 'em happy, reckon?"

"Maybe. But we need to stay wary," answered Gabe, returning to his task.

***

With the dressed-out carcass over his shoulders, Gabe and Ezra started to the camp, pausing only to pick up the turkey as they passed the brush. Within moments, they were greeted by the women, worried looks on their faces as Otter asked, "You heard the wolves?"

"Yeah, but they'll prob'ly be happy with the gut pile we left 'em."

"If there are many, they might want more," countered Otter.

"We'll keep a good fire goin', keep the horses in close, it'll be alright," suggested Ezra, accepting a cup of coffee from Dove.

Otter glanced at Ezra, back at Gabe, then dropped her eyes and started dishing up their evening fare, a stew of smoked meat, timpsila, skunk cabbage, and more. With fresh corn biscuits to sop up the juices, the men were happy with the offering and were soon sitting back enjoying their coffee. The women had already started deboning the deer, cutting thin strips to smoke, and wrapping choice cuts in big plantain leaves to pack in the parfleche. Intermittent howls of the wolves told them the pack was near, each howl answered by the squeaking attempt at a howl by the pup.

"Sounds like they're busy with the gut pile," suggested Gabe.

"If they were busy, they wouldn't be howling. Fighting maybe, but not those howls we're hearing. They might be gathering the rest of the pack together," answered Ezra, holding his cup near his chin as he spoke quietly to Gabe, not wanting to alarm the women.

But the women were more seasoned in the mountains than the men and with each eerie howl that was answered from a distance, they looked at one another, knowingly. Otter walked to Gabe, "You should have your weapons ready. They," pointing into the deepening darkness, "will be coming."

"You think so?" asked Gabe, sitting up and listening to the cry of the wild.

"Yes. They are gathering the pack. It is because of the smell of blood and meat. Unless there is some other kill nearby, this is what they want," she explained, pointing at the strips of meat that lay on the log.

"Ezra, let's get all our firepower ready, then we'll gather more wood for the fire." He turned back to Otter, "You women get your rifles also. Check the loads and have 'em ready here, by the log."

He glanced at the horses, Ebony and the mustangs were already showing skittish, but the others, though wary, were not displaying any nervousness. Ebony stood, head high, ears twitching back and forth, eyes wide as he watched the darkness, looking in the direction of the river where the men killed the deer. Gabe walked over to the big stallion, stroked his neck and head, speaking softly to him, encouraging the big black. He stepped away, picked up his two saddle pistols and the Ferguson rifle and brought them closer to the fire. Both Gabe and Ezra quickly checked each of the weapons, ensuring flash pans were primed and shut, and hammers at half-cock.

Ezra finished first and started to the tree line, breaking off the dead limbs within arm's reach, picking up broken branches, making an armful and returned to the fire. Within moments the pile of firewood grew with the addition of a couple smaller snags that would be fed to the fire as they burned.

The women had quit the butchering and now stood watching the tree line for any sign of the wolves, staying on guard as the men finished with the wood gathering and picketing the horses. Gabe wanted each of the horses to have room to fight if necessary and gave ample lead to the picket for each one. The ties were secure, ensuring the horses would not just panic and run making themselves prime targets for the pack that would quickly hamstring them and take them down, where the pack would overwhelm them.

The howls had gone silent. Otter looked at Gabe, "They're coming."

Each one scanned the trees, knowing the firelight would be reflected in the eyes of any of the wolves, revealing their whereabouts before the light would shine into the darkness of the thin woods against black and grey coats. They were surrounded by juniper and piñon. Trees that were good for wind breaks and cover against being seen, but the low hanging branches and thick needle bearing limbs reduced their visibility and offered cover for the attackers.

"There!" shouted Dove as her rifle spat flame into the darkness. A whine came from the blackness, telling of a wounded animal. Dove dropped the butt of her rifle to the ground and busied herself reloading. Then the wolves were everywhere.

A monstrous grey beast soared from the trees directly at Gabe. Teeth bared, slobbers flying, eyes flaring orange in the firelight, the ruff on his neck making him look as big as a bear with his paws stretched forward, the beast launched himself. Gabe lifted the muzzle of his rifle toward the ogre and pulled the trigger. The big .62 caliber ball met the lunge and pierced the chest, blossoming red, but the impetus of the lunge carried the beast into the face of Gabe, knocking him to his back. Gabe instantly rolled out from under the quivering mass of grey, saw the beast was in the throes of death and turned to the trees, searching for another target. He stood, frantically reloading the rifle almost from memory and feel, as he watched the trees.

A rifle roared at his side. Ezra had scored a hit on a thin-sided grey before it started his leap. Ebony screamed, reared, and came down with both front hooves driving into the head and shoulders of a black wolf that snarled and tried to bite, but whimpered when the hooves broke its neck and opened his chest. Ebony shook his head, stepped back, glared at the dying beast and lifted his eyes to see another wolf, more wary, and trying to circle the big stallion. The canine looked at the steeldust mustang, who pranced side to side, baring his teeth, and shaking his head. The wolf chose the mustang and lowered his head as he neared, the steeldust watching and waiting. The mustang anticipated the wolf's lunge, swung around and caught the animal mid-lunge with both hind feet and sent him caterwauling end over end to the edge of the fire which flared and scorched the entire side of the attacker. The wolf, dragging one hind leg, head hanging, tail tucked, dragged himself from the fight.

His rifle loaded, Gabe leaned it on the log and snatched up both saddle pistols. The double barreled

.52 caliber pistols with their thirteen-inch barrels, were deadly at close quarters and he believed he needed the firepower. He had no sooner turned, than a black form hurtled itself at him, but Gabe instantly brought both hammers to full cock, and discharged both barrels at the beast. He was surprised that the first sensation was of burning hair, but the double blast stopped the wolf mid-flight, and felled him at the feet of the shooter. Blood surged from the wolf's neck and Gabe kicked away the carcass.

Suddenly, Otter's rifle roared, but the beast she shot at was still coming. Gabe threw himself toward her, firing his second pistol as he leaped. He scored a hit, but the wolf hit the ground and turned, head down, bloody slobbers dripping from his wide mouth that showed bloody teeth. Orange eyes glared as he lifted one grey paw, stretching it toward his prey, then the next. Gabe brought the second hammer to full cock, the sound of metal against metal loud in the darkness. The wolf glanced at Gabe, turned back to face the woman who was hurriedly loading her rifle, then he tensed, leaned back slightly and started his lunge. Gabe fired, the bullet hitting the wolf in the neck and stopping his leap as he fell at the feet of Otter, who had not backed up a step but stood her ground. She primed the pan, cocked and set the trigger and brought the rifle to full cock without moving her eyes from the wolf at her feet. Satisfied the beast was dead, she turned her eyes to the tree line, searching for another.

Gabe returned to his place, busied himself with reloading the pistols as he watched the trees, listening for sounds of attack. One was loaded, he worked at the second, loading both barrels and priming both locks, never taking his eyes from the trees. Once they were done, he sat them on the log, and lifted his Ferguson, searching the entire camp. The only sounds were the low rumble from Ebony as he shook his head side to side, prancing, wanting to fight, and the crackling of the fire, sending sparks skyward.

Slowly, they gathered closer together, sat on the two logs before the fire, but with their backs to the fire and eyes on the woods. Scattered around the camp were the bodies of five wolves. As Gabe looked at each one, he commented, "Seems like we got more'n that."

"I saw a couple limp off into the trees," explained Ezra.

"One of them, the one the mustang kicked, lost most of his hair in the fire and he ran off," offered Dove.

"I don't think they'll try that again," offered Gabe, looking at Otter.

"No, I do not think they will. But it would be best to keep watch," she answered.

Gabe chuckled, "I'm not partial to goin' to sleep

anyway. I'll keep watch."

Otter reached for the larger parfleche and pulled the pup from within. He wagged his tail and licked the face of the woman, happy to be free from his hideout. Otter smiled, stretched him on her lap and stroked his fur.

Gabe said, "Almost hard to believe that he's just like them," nodding to the dead wolves.

No one spoke or moved, harboring their own thoughts, until Ezra pushed the coffee pot closer to the fire, then added, "Reckon I'll be sittin' up with you."

8 / Raid

They turned their back on what they considered were the meager offerings and limited temptations of both Hudson's Bay Company and the Northwest Company. With Hudson's having a virtual monopoly on the fur trade in Rupert's Land and the northwest of Spanish Louisiana and Canada, the Northwest Company controlled the fur trade south of Rupert's Land and in the northern Rockies east to the Mississippi River, or land that would one day be the northern reaches of the United States. The Coureur des bois were independent entrepreneurs who took or traded for furs and sold them to the companies. But they were at a distinct disadvantage to the companies who set the prices for each fur and brokered no argument. Each of the men had spent their time with the companies, exploring, trading and more, but were now determined to make their own way without the binding restrictions of fur companies or laws, what there were, of the land.

Jacques Beauchamp, the self-appointed leader, had gained additional followers as the band of renegades and blackguards traveled southwest from Grand Portage and forced their will upon all they came upon. Before they were joined by the newcomers, Beauchamp and his four followers had hit Munier's and Petit's Ponca posts at the confluence of the Niobrara and Missouri Rivers. Several of the workers were killed, some Ponca traders, and Petit's post was burned, but only after both posts had been ransacked by Beauchamp's band. It was less than a week after the raid on the posts that three men hailed their camp and soon joined the band. The three were led by Elijah "Smitty" Smith, an American who had tried his hand with the Northwest company and was discharged after a bloody fight with an Arikara sub-chief. His friend, Jesse Finlay, who had been sent packing by Northwest for trying to cash in on furs stolen from the Mandan village, had become his comrade-in-arms. But the most intimidating of the three was Rupert Beaulieux, a former Voyageur with Hudson's Bay company. A big man standing four inches over six feet and almost as broad as he was tall, his bushy beard covered the tree stump neck and the woolen shirt strained at the shoulders, chest and arms from the mass of muscles hidden underneath. Beaulieux was a surly man and seldom spoke, shoving his way through life with his bulk, the only time he showed any concern was for his horse, a cross-breed Percheron that looked like he belonged behind a wagon or a plow, but beside his rider, the two were as companionable as could be, always concerned for the other.

Once they left the Ponca posts, Beauchamp had hired the guide, Crow's Heart, a Mandan who sported the unusual deep auburn hair and blue eyes typical of their Norse heritage, but the dark complexion of the Mandan. Within a week, Beauchamp had also recruited two renegade natives, a Miniconjou, Hewáia, Lone Horn, and an Assiniboine, Watopachnato, Big Devil. Now numbering eleven well-armed and experienced men, Beauchamp believed they had a band that could exert their will whenever and wherever needed, and he began to make plans for his excursion to follow the Missouri River into the land of the Arikara, Mandan, Hidatsa, Assiniboin, and if possible, to take the Yellowstone into the Crow country.

Crow's Heart, the Mandan guide and scout, rode from the trees toward Beauchamp, stopped and waited from the man to come near. "Village," he held up both hands, all fingers extended, flashed them three times, "this many. Old people, little children. Men gone on buffalo hunt."

Jacques grinned at the report, "How far?"

"Two fingers," he answered, nodding at the sun.

Jacques knew that would be about a half hour, ample time to make a plan. He pulled to the side, motioned the others near, and began, "There's a village up yonder and we're gonna take it. Crow's Heart says it about thirty lodges, but the men and women are gone. Just a bunch of old people and kids. So, here's what we're gonna do." He began to lay out his plan of attack and assigned duties to each man. The two renegade natives would go with Crow's Heart and station themselves to watch for the return of the hunters, then take any horses that could be found. He split up the rest of the men, four leading the attack, killing any that armed themselves. The remaining three would ransack each of the lodges and would be joined by the attackers from the other end of the village.

"We need to get this done in a hurry. Take only pelts and buff'ler robes, ain't gonna be packin' any souvenirs, got that?" he snarled at the group.

Nodding heads gave him his answer and he reined around, saying over his shoulder, "Then let's get goin'. This is just the first of many!"

The village lay in a broad meadow set back from the bank of the Missouri just downstream from the Knife River. Trees were abundant on the north edge, but their approach came from the south and the scattered trees offered little coverage. A slight slope led to the crest of the only mound or hill anywhere near. Jacques saw the two renegades swing wide and start to the crest of the hill. It was less than two hundred yards from the tree line to the village, and Beauchamp chose to ride slowly toward the village, wanting the Arikara people to think they were traders coming to barter. As they drew near, Jacques motioned to the men to split up, and with a shout he led the four directly into the village at a run. As they passed the first lodge, an old woman ducked behind the entry blanket, taking shelter within the earth mound lodge. An old man stepped in front of Jacques only to be run down by the horses, leaving his trampled body bleeding in the dirt. A young woman stepped out and brought up a bow and nocked arrow, but as she started the draw, Marchand shot her with his pistol, never slowing his horse as he passed, watching her fall with blood spreading on her chest.

Within moments they were through the village, leaving behind at least five dead, either trampled or shot. The four swung their horses around as Beauchamp barked, "Me'n Ducette will ride through the lodges, you two start gatherin' up the pelts!" Marchand and Moreau reined their mounts around and started for the nearest lodges.

The men separated, entering the lodges at will.

Occasionally a shot was heard, or a scream or shouts, as the lodges were looted, and the village plundered. Within less than half an hour, the men were gathering at the north end of the villages, horses loaded with pelts and robes, men laughing and telling the stories of their encounters. "I was hopin' to find me a good lookin' squaw, but ever one I seen was old 'nuff to be muh mother!" declared Smitty, laughing.

Crow's Heart, Lone Horn, and Big Devil rode up, each leading three horses that were quickly grabbed and loaded by the raiders. At Beauchamp's signal, the entire band rode away from the village, hooting and hollering as they disappeared into the trees. After a few miles, Beauchamp reined up and turned to the men. "We need to make time, but we've got to spare the horses. Don't know when the men from that village will return and if they'll come after us, but we've got enough daylight to make another ten miles or so, then we'll camp. You might be feelin' good with what we got, but this is just the beginning. By the time we head back down the Missouri, I 'spect we'll each be leading a line of pack horses of six or more. That means each man could be haulin' a fortune!" The band broke into cheers and shouts at the thought of having a fortune and doing very little work to get it, not counting the killing and packing, but it was what the men wanted to hear, and they were looking forward to the prize.

None thought of the killing, considering only the bounty. Nor were their thoughts about the villages destroyed, lives ruined, and damage done. Such is the way of the laggard and ne'er do well, the murderer and the thief, those of evil bent thought only of themselves and what they would gain, regardless of the cost to others. But Vengeance is mine, I will repay, saith the Lord.

9 / Absaroka

The eastern sky blushed a pale gold that faded to a dusty soft blue as the first light of day pushed back the tide of darkness to silhouette the jagged horizon behind the travelers. They had an early start with little sleep from the night with the wolves and were anxious to put the wilderness battle behind them, pushing toward the craggy Absaroka mountains that stood sentinel on the northeastern edge of the Wind River valley. With the Wind River Mountains off their left shoulder, they followed the meandering Wind River that came from the higher mountains directly to the west. The broad shoulders of the wide valley began to push together, and the surrounding terrain showed considerable contrast. To the north, the adobe hills were scarred by numerous runoff ravines and smaller gullies, exposing the myriad of colors of the clay-like soil that bore patches of prickly pear and scattered cholla and yucca cacti. While the south flats rose to dark timbered shoulders with steep sided ravines marked by limestone cliffs and piñons with tenuous toeholds hoarding their luscious nuts in sap covered cones, all framed by the black timbered slopes that led to the granite tipped mountains of the Wind River Range.

Gabe breathed deep of the clear mountain air, tinted by the pines with the mild but sweet fragrance from random blossoms of sego lily, chokecherry, and the golden pea. But another scent caught his attention, one he recognized just before they rounded a bend to come upon a small herd of big horn mountain sheep. Two big rams stood staring at the newcomers to their valley, massive horns curled into a full circle, brown turning darker at narrow tips. Black eyes glared accenting the only white that framed the black nose. Broad chests above narrow agile limbs with the only movement a slight puff of wind stirring the warm coats of hollow hair. The bigger of the two with a single broken tip on his horns, visibly relaxed, started chewing his cud, paused, and dropped his head for another bite of grass. Six ewes, several staring, started moving when the herd ram relaxed, and pushed their lambs closer to the water. Three younger rams cavorted on the far side of the herd, practicing their jousting skills, butting one another playfully.

Gabe and company had reined up to watch the herd, enjoying the sight of so many up close. When he gigged Ebony forward, the big rams alerted the herd and within seconds the entire bunch had disappeared up one of the steep rocky hillsides. When high up and in an almost inaccessible spot, the lead ewe stopped and looked back at the strange group on the valley floor. Satisfied they were in no danger; she led the herd higher still and soon disappeared into a rocky crevasse.

Gabe looked back at Ezra, grinning, "God sure is somethin', ain't He?"

Ezra was also grinning as he watched the white rumps disappear, turned to Gabe, "Yes, He is!"

Gabe noticed Otter had a puzzled look on her face, but she said nothing, and he knew it best to wait for her to voice her concern or opinion, without any badgering from him. The hillsides to their left had an orange tint to the clay that set them apart from that on the far side and what they had already encountered. Narrow bands of sandstone marked the hills as layered with deep courses of clay-like soil between each strip of sandstone. They rounded a long finger that pushed into the river from the far side, then crossed a low peninsula where the river cut back on itself, when the valley opened up to reveal a confluence of two forks of the Wind River. One cut through the dry land to the north, the other marking their way west. Gabe motioned for them to stop when he came to a wide flat shoulder with ample grass for the horses. It was time for a mid-day break to give the horses a breather and to take some much-needed rest for themselves.

When they stepped down, Otter looked at Gabe, "Tell me about your God."

Gabe grinned as he loosened the girth on Ebony, walked to the pack horse and over his shoulder, answered, "Be happy to, but let's get us some food 'fore we start that. It might take a while."

Otter smiled, nodded, and having finished with her horse, started gathering some sticks for a small cookfire. In a short while, lunch was over, and the four sat with their cups of hot brew when Otter said, "Tell me."

Gabe grinned, dropped to the ground beside a boulder, leaned back and began, "In the beginning, there was nothing but darkness. So God stood upon nothing, cuz there was nothing to stand on, and began creating. After he began, He said, 'Let there be light!' and so there was, and He called the light, day, and the dark, night. Then He looked at what he had, decided to shape things up a little and separated that part," he pointed at the sky, "from this part," pointing at the ground. "He called that," pointing at the sky, "Heaven, and this He called earth. Then He started shaping things, you know, pushing up the mountains, leveling out the plains, moving the water into lakes and rivers and the oceans. Then he looked around and figgered things could use a little decoratin' and spread the trees, flowers, grasses and such like and stood aside, put his hands on His hips and said, 'That's good!'"

Dove and Otter looked at one another, smiling, then back at Gabe, waiting for him to continue.

"Then He set the sun in the sky and the moon and said for the greater light to rule the day and the lesser light to rule the night. And then he flung the stars," he gave a throwing motion with one arm, "into the night sky so we could find our way at night. Then he created the fish in the waters, the birds in the sky, and all the animals on the land. Then came the hard part. He created man, then He took a rib," pointing to his own rib, "from man and made woman. He said they were to have the rule over everything! Then He stood back and said," Gabe paused and nodded to Ezra who finished with, "That is very good!"

Both men grinned, chuckling, and looked at the women. Ezra asked, "So, what do you think?"

"I like your creation story," declared Dove, enthusiastically, then looked at Otter who nodded her agreement, smiling.

"Then comes the best part," added Gabe. "He did all that in six days, then He said, It's time to rest'." Gabe slid down the boulder, turned to his side and put an arm under his head and closed his eyes. The others chuckled and followed his example. It had been a long and tiresome night with the wolf pack attack, and no one needed extra encouragement to take a short nap.

***

By the end of the second day out from the wolf pack attack site, they came to another confluence of streams. "The Wind River's gettin' mighty small!" declared Ezra as he looked at the dwindling stream. Although flowing clear as it chuckled its way through the chokecherries and service berries, it still crashed over the rocks and spread about forty to fifty feet wide. But the feeder stream showed itself to be about the same width and depth, while it came from a wide, flat valley that showed a tall mountain standing at the far end, its timber covered shoulders lifting a bare peak high above its neighbors.

Gabe looked around, nodded toward a flat top long butte on the east side of the valley and said, "Let's take a look from up there." He pointed Ebony to a faint trail that sidled the slope to the top and started the ascent. The flat top butte stood about four hundred feet above the valley floor and gave the explorers a panoramic view of their surroundings. To the south, stretching from the west to the east, stood the long range of the Wind River Mountains, craggy peaks marching to the east to disappear into the flats. North rose the Absaroka Range, standing guard on both sides of the valley, intimidating with their jagged needle pointed peaks appearing to hold the very heavens aloft.

Gabe looked around, amazed at the wonder and the distance they could see, having never before even imagined such a marvelous piece of God's creation. He grinned at Ezra, then looked down to Otter, "What can you tell us about this place?"

She pointed with her chin to the long butte across the valley, "The Wind River has its start beyond those mountains. Far beyond is the land of thunder and the home of the Blackfoot and Gros Ventre." Gabe stared into the distance, seeing the low passage between the two mountain ranges, nodded and looked at her again. She turned to her right, pointed up the wide valley, "Those are the Absaroka Mountains, because that is the land of the Crow. This valley is a land of much game, elk, bear, deer, moose, and more."

"What do you mean, 'the land of thunder'?" he asked.

"The land has many strange things. Most consider it a place of the gods. Water comes from the ground, high up!" She motioned by pointing high above her head and looking up. "There are strange things, some of the water holes are hot, animals die there. When the water shoots high, it sounds like thunder."

Gabe looked at Ezra, "Think that might be something to remember. Maybe explore it some other time. Right now, I'm thinkin' this is the way to go. What'chu think?" he asked, pointing up the wide valley to the north.

"Suits me," answered Ezra, grinning at Dove. "Long's we're together, we can go anywhere!"

Gabe grinned, nodded, and started off the butte to make camp near the stream. "I think I'd like some fish for supper, anybody else?" He looked back at the others and Otter answered for them, "Yes!" She stroked the scruff of Wolf as he straddled the saddle before her, "And Wolf says yes!"

"Then fish it is!" declared Gabe, looking below at a likely campsite by the stream.

10 / Raiders

"Look, when we were with Mackenzie, he got most of his information from some Canadian trappers and traders. I was there when he was talkin' to James Mackay, one o' them traders, and he was tellin' him all about the Missouri River, an' I listened real close," explained Beauchamp. He was seated by the fire with Ducette and Marchand, discussing their plans and routes. "The Missouri bends to the south after a long stretch, now I ain't been that far, but Mackenzie sent some of us to scout it out and meet back up with him on the Souris. He had some maps that came from the Spanish, but it was a Frenchman that was responsible, a Jean Baptiste Truteau. But them maps weren't no good for where we was. Ya see, on the south side o' the river, there's a couple others, the Yellowstone and the Shoshone, accordin' to what Truteau said, but what we found was the Yellowstone had a fork, and the Shoshone ain't too far from it. And that there's Crow country and they's good hunters and such. Now, here's what I'm thinkin'."

He leaned toward the men, snatched up a stick and began to draw in the dirt at their feet. "The Missouri runs west to east along here, and the Yellowstone feeds from the south here, and down this away it forks. Now, if we come down the Yellowstone, take this south fork, then we can cut cross country and hit the Shoshone, follow it back to the Missouri and then start for St. Louis or New Orleans!" He sat back, grinning and watching the reaction of the men.

"But will we have a good load by that time?" asked Marchand, looking past the glare of the fire to the leader of the group.

"We're 'bout through the Assiniboine country, got us some stuff. But the Crow, they're better hunters and they're nearer the mountains and should have a lot more pelts. Now, we got us some buffler, deer, elk, lynx, an' such, but the Crow'll have more beaver, and there's more money in beaver." He leaned toward his map, "All this country is Crow, closer to the mountains, but easy goin' too. So, I figger by the time we make this loop, we should be loaded with 'bout all we can handle. When we get back to the Missouri, we'll hafta decide if we're gonna make rafts or get some canoes, or what we're gonna do to get 'em downriver, but we can work that out later."

"So, you think we'll have a good load, but just what is a good load for you?" asked Ducette. Although he knew Beauchamp better than the others, he wanted the details. He was, after all, putting his life on the line just like the others and it was his life, his future, they were gambling on and he wanted more certainty.

"Well, if every man has two or three pack horses loaded when we get back to the Missouri, I figger that'll be a good load. That'd be a pack train of twenty-five to thirty pack horses, loaded heavy. Say, two bundles of furs each, that'd be about five hundred dollars per horse. So, we're talkin' in the range of close to fifteen thousand dollars!"

"Wheeooo," whistled Ducette. "But, by the time we split it among ever'body, that ain't so much!"

Beauchamp dropped his eyes, chuckled and looked back at the two men, "Maybe the Crow will help with that."

"Whatchu mean," rasped Ducette, leaning forward, eyes squinting.

"We been lucky so far, ain't had to go against any big bunch o' warriors, but them Crow, they's different. It just might be that by the time we're back to the Missouri, there won't be so many of us." He leaned toward the two men, lowered his voice and added, "An' them Injuns, they ain't gettin' a full share anyway. Couple o' jugs will make them happy."

The men sat back, Marchand stirring the coals

with a stick before adding another log. He looked at Beauchamp, "How long you think this loop'll take us?"

"Well, we're a couple days away from crossin' over and takin' the Yellowstone, then I figger a couple weeks, thereabouts, 'fore we get back to the Missouri. But that'll give us plenty time to get the furs to St. Louis or farther, 'fore the snow flies," answered Beauchamp, digging for the makings for his pipe. "Now, I was figgerin' on the low side, if we get a good price on them pelts, it could be twict that much!" He lit the pipe, took a deep draw, and sat back, satisfied with his spiel.

The men also sat back, staring into the flames, imagining what they could do with their share that could amount to as much as two thousand dollars. In a time when a farm or a small general store could be bought for a thousand dollars, the men smiled as their imaginations began to take them where they had never gone before.

***

Gabe and company kept to a game trail that followed the east edge of the wide valley, hugging the bottom of the slopes that bordered the green bottom. The small river twisted and wound its way back and forth across the valley floor, choosing its own route that showed to be different with every season. Many were the gravelly beds formerly used by the river until it found an easier way, leaving behind a combination of gravel beds and mud bogs sprouting cattails. The shadows of the eastern ridges stretched across the green riverbed slowly withdrawing as the sun rose in the east. The travelers were in the dim shadows and moved silently save the creak of saddle leather and the occasional clatter of hooves against the loose stones.

It was proving to be a land of plenty, with less than three miles on their start, they spotted a huge herd of elk, probably well over a hundred, grazing in the valley bottom. The cows were protective of spindly legged orange colored calves and the bulls just beginning to show velvet covered spikes that would eventually become massive antlers that arched over their backs. The wapiti paid little attention to the small group of travelers across the river from their graze and continued with their morning activities without concern. Otter pointed out a pair of cows nursing new offspring while a couple of older calves cavorted as they tried out their new legs.

Several small family groups of mule deer walked to the water but keeping watch on the intruders to their land. They too had youngsters, spotted coats and skinny legs, bounding beside them, big ears flopping as they frolicked. Otter pointed to the far slope, "Bear," where a black bear with twin cubs walked across the face of the hillside, occasionally turning over some logs that had been felled by some long-time-ago fire, looking for grubs. Gabe reined up when he saw several horse tracks that cut their trail. He motioned to the tracks, stepped down for a closer look and saw Otter also dismount to join him. As he walked forward, he also looked up the nearby slope and around the trail and valley for any giveaway of visitors. Otter dropped to one knee, looking closely at the sign, then looked at Gabe, "Wild horses. They have colts and yearlings with them, none have riders."

"That's a relief. I'm not in the mood for a fight," declared Gabe, also on one knee examining the tracks. He looked at Otter, "This is beautiful country, but we're getting close to Crow lands aren't we?"

"Yes. But there are many others that come into these lands to raid other villages. It is the way of the people," answered Otter, standing.

Gabe also stood, looked at Otter, "Yeah, I know that. We've seen it among the Shawnee, Chickasaw, Quapaw, Osage, Missouri, Kansa, Oto, and others. Seems like everywhere we go, there's one or more bands that are enemies with another and fighting for their lands or something. Everybody raiding everybody else, but I guess it's not much different with the white man. Our people were at war with the

British, now the British and the French are at war, and so it goes, all over the world. That's one of the reasons Ezra and I came west, to get away from all that, but . . ." he let the thought hang between them, then nodded for her to mount and he did the same.

Mid-morning their trail was broken by a timber covered draw that split the hills on the east and lay in the shadow of a tall granite peak bordered on either side by sawtooth ridges. The draw held a dry creek bed that had at some time carried an abundance of gravel and sand to form an alluvial fan across the valley bottom, literally splitting the valley in two. The draw was dimpled with big boulders and marked by many piñon trees and an occasional cedar showing a tint of blue. They pushed on across the slight rise and continued into the upper valley.

It was approaching mid-day and Gabe was feeling a little uncomfortable. He stood in his stirrups, looking over the valley floor. Here the stream had kept to its lower bed and the grassy meadows on either side were tempting fields for game. There were elk, deer, a small group of antelope, all grazing contentedly, but nothing that caused concern. Yet the hair on his neck was standing stiff, and he always heeded those feelings. He looked back at Ezra, saw him scanning the area as well, then with a glance to Gabe, he nodded, affirming he was having the same intimations. Gabe dropped into his seat and having spotted a dry creek leading into the valley, pointed Ebony alongside. They were at the head of the valley; four creeks fed the small river and Otter had said they would take the cut to the northeast. They had passed the larger of the four, choosing instead to take the better choice of the dry creek that held ample grass and tree cover if needed.

The ravine switched back on itself, then opened into a hanging valley about a quarter mile wide and less than a mile long. A small spring fed creek came from a little pond in the middle of the meadow. Junipers, piñons, and cedar trees surrounded the haven and Gabe chose it for their mid-day break. He had just dropped to the ground and asked Otter to take care of Ebony as he slipped the scope from his saddle bags and pulled the Ferguson from the scabbard. "I'm goin' up on that knob at the mouth of the ravine and look around. Somethin's not right and I think we might be gettin' visitors." With a nod, Ezra slipped his Lancaster from the scabbard, pulled his war club from beneath the fender on the other side, and started after Gabe.

Otter nodded and went to work on the horses, loosening their girths, slipping the parfleche of foodstuffs from the pack, and motioned for Dove to do likewise. They would have a cold camp, and the women worked diligently laying things out in the shade of a couple of big junipers, to await the men.

Otter spoke quietly to Dove, "I will go to Gabe. You stay with the horses," and turned away before Dove could object.

Blackfoot!" whispered Otter from behind Gabe. Her man jumped slightly, turned to look back at his woman, shaking his head. He turned back, still on his belly, lifted the glass to his eye and whispered, "How can you tell?"

"Their horses, their feathers. Blackfoot. Raiding party, not hunters. No horses to pack meat," explained Otter.

Gabe looked and when Otter touched his back he knew she wanted to see also and handed her the scope. She lifted the scope and adjusted it, then whispered, "That may be Back Fat, their chief. He is a big man."

"Back Fat? What kind of name is that?" asked Gabe.

"Buffalo Bull's Back Fat is his name," answered Otter, returning the scope to her man.

"Well, no matter who he is, we better get back to our camp and get ready in case they come across our sign and come after us," stated Ezra, crabbing back away from the edge of the knob.

Gabe slid back and came to his feet beside Otter, "Let's do as he said. No time to waste!"

11 / Pass

Gabe quickly chose the positions for the women where the ravine cut back on itself. The men walked them to their positions, stationing each one near a sizable juniper, Otter on the south rim, Dove on the north, both with their rifles and accouterments. Gabe and Ezra met at the bottom of the ravine where it cut back to the north, bending around a talus slope that offered good protection for the two men. Gabe chose his Mongol bow, his over/under pistol in his belt, while Ezra preferred his Lancaster rifle, his double-barreled pistol in his belt and his war club at his side. Ezra had stripped down to reveal his bare torso that bulged and rippled with muscles from his broad shoulders to his deep chest and massive arms, the sight of which would be intimidating to any opponent. He flexed his muscles, hefted his war club and swung it overhead, making it whistle through the air, then looked at Gabe, grinning, "I'm ready, you?"

Gabe had strung his bow, nocked an arrow and had two more stuck in the ground at his feet. He grinned at his partner, nodded, "Yup."

They looked down the ravine, waiting for the coming of the Blackfoot warriors. They had not waited to see if their tracks had been found, nor to see if the band or any of the warriors had chosen to pursue the sign. For any skilled tracker, it was obvious there were six horses, all loaded or ridden, and the thought of taking that many horses alone would be tempting to any raiders.

Gabe's plan was to confront the warriors, giving them an opportunity to pass on this encounter that would be costly to both parties, and hoped the chief, Buffalo Bull's Back Fat, would be wise enough to count the cost. The two men stood about eight feet apart, feet widespread, their firm resolve painting their faces with stern expressions, each man breathed deeply as they heard the clatter of hooves on the trail.

Four warriors pulled up at the sight of the two men standing together in the middle of the narrow ravine. They knew these men waited for battle and would not move unless defeated. Gabe shouted, "You choose! Leave and live! Stay and die!" As he spoke, Ezra used signs to translate.

It was evident the four understood, if not the

exact words, but at least the intent. They looked at one another, argued, gestured toward the men, then decided.

Gabe said, "Here they come. I'll take that leader with the lance; you take the one with the shield."

The four leaned forward on their horses' necks, kicked them to a lunging charge, and they came screaming their war cries, eyes glaring. The ravine was only wide enough for them to charge two by two, and Gabe and Ezra were ready. They waited, waited, then at Gabe's release, his arrow flew true to its mark, taking the lance bearer just under the chin and lifting him from his horse to fall to the ground to be trampled by the man directly behind him. Ezra's Lancaster barked, spitting fire, smoke and lead, wrapping Ezra's head in a thin cloud of grey smoke. The bullet split the warrior's shield, shattered his arm, and buried itself in the warrior's chest. The man dropped his bow, clung to the mane of his horse, jerking the animal to the side.

Gabe nocked his second arrow and Ezra lifted his war club as the two remaining warriors kept coming. The warrior under Gabe's arrow was sitting erect, drawing his own bow but before he could release the shaft, Gabe's arrow split his breastbone and buried itself to the fletching. The warrior slumped forward, releasing his arrow which clattered to the ground, legs grasping the horse and his hands jerking at the mane, but he slid to the side and tumbled end over end, stopping within a foot of Gabe. Ezra's war club was bloody from striking the passing warrior that sought to take him with a lance. Ezra had sidestepped as he swung and the halberd blade on his war club sliced off the back of the warrior's skull, spilling his bloody brains down his back as he nosedived into the dirt.

Both men glanced at their adversaries, noting three were dead, one still clinging to his horse's mane, his bloody arm and side dripping red down his leg to drip on the shattered shield. He looked at the two men before him, slowly shook his head, and used his one good arm to rein his horse around and start back down the ravine. Neither Gabe nor Ezra moved to stop him, both hoping he would discourage the others from coming into the ravine.

"We've got time. Let's put some distance between us an' them," suggested Gabe. He waved the women down and started back to the horses. They hoped the Blackfoot would choose to leave but suspected they would instead seek vengeance. Within moments, all were mounted and on the move, kicking their mounts to a canter toward what Otter had called a mountain pass that would take them to the Shoshone River and beyond.

Gabe motioned for Otter to take the lead as they cleared the hanging valley and ducked into the black timber. They slowed to a walk, but Otter kicked up the pace at every clearing, opening or other opportunity. The narrow trail rounded a rimrock knob that overhung the trail like a prehistoric ogre searching for its next prey. The shadow hid the trail only slightly and the four wove in and out of the timber, keeping a steady pace. The trail dropped into a ravine, thick with brush and timber and with the constant urging of their riders the horses crashed through the thicket and broke into a small meadow. The path sloped up the meadow, following the narrow stream that chuckled over the rocks, cascaded over short waterfalls and sought escape from the high country. Just before they went into the timber, Gabe reined up and swung around in his saddle for a quick look at their back-trail. He saw movement in the trees below and he stood in his stirrups, shading his squinted eyes for a better look below. He looked at Ezra, mouthed the words, "They're comin'!" and turned Ebony to catch up with Otter.

They hit another small meadow and Otter reined up, pointing ahead at a low saddle marked by a break in a long line of rimrock that swooped down from the taller mountains. "There is where we cross!"

"Then we better hurry, those Blackfoot are comin' fast!" answered Gabe.

Otter looked back, turned quickly and slapped legs against the sides of her blue roan, leaning down and encouraging the animal as they headed once again into the black timber. The trail twisted through the timber following the ravine that fed the headwaters of the small creek. Another clearing gave a brief reprieve and Otter reined up. She looked at Gabe, "The horses need a breather before we start that climb," pointing to the steep hillside littered with dead trees that had fallen in a blowdown some years prior.

"There's a trail there?" asked Gabe, searching the timber.

"Yes, it is steep, but we can make it. It cuts back on itself there!" pointing about half way up the steep slope. "The worst part is just below the crest, we might have to lead the horses over," she warned.

Ezra and Dove had come alongside, listening and looking. Ezra asked, "Is there any other way over?"

Dove looked at her man, "No, not for many miles. Several days travel."

Gabe heard Dove's comment and turned to Ezra, "Those Blackfoot are gettin' mighty close. Once I'm on top, I'm gonna take cover above that rimrock that overlooks this whole valley. I want you to take the packhorses and the women and get 'em clear of this. I can keep 'em busy and away from the pass here. Prob'ly discourage 'em from followin'. Then I'll catch up with you."

"The women can make it alright. I'll stay with you

and double the firepower," offered Ezra.

"No, I'd rather you be with the women, just in case."

"Just in case you don't make it, you mean?" said Ezra, quietly.

"Ummhmmm, somethin' like that. But, I ain't plannin' on not makin' it!" declared Gabe.

Otter led off and the entourage started the side slope climb to the narrow saddle that crossed over the ridge. At the first switchback, the sorrel packhorse slipped on the shale, staggered, but Gabe's taut lead rope gave it the needed anchor and it soon found footing and pushed up against Ebony's rump, crowding the black up the trail. Then true to Otter's prediction, the last few yards were steeper and crossed unstable slide rock and she was the first to step down and start up the vertical rocky slope, using toes, knees, and hands to make the climb, keeping a taut lead on her blue roan.

Gabe tied off the lead for the sorrel packhorse to the pommel of his saddle, stepped down and started up the climb, Ebony staying close behind as if afraid he would be left behind if he didn't stay close, and with every step, the sorrel stayed with them. Within a few tiring moments, they crossed the saddle, everyone flopping on their backs to catch their breath in the high-altitude thin air. His chest heaving, Gabe struggled to sit up, looked below and saw the war party coming on as they broke from the trees into the lower meadow. He looked to Ezra, "You all need to get a move on, rest up a ways down the trail. And I've got to get in position." He stood, handing the lead rope of the sorrel to Otter, then embraced her quickly, "You and Dove go with Ezra. I'm gonna hold these Blackfoot off, see if I can discourage 'em a mite." He reached to her head, fingered a yellow ribbon she had, and untied it, "I think I might use this," he said, grinning. He reached down and rubbed Wolf behind the ears, giving a passing thought to how fast the pup had grown, almost fully grown now. "You take care of 'em now, y'hear," he said to the Wolf, who stared at the man, unmoving.

He led Ebony to a small piñon and loosely tethered him with a slip knot, as usual, to ensure that if necessary the horse could pull himself free and escape. He saw his friends round the bend of the wide ravine that would lead them to the headwaters of the Shoshone and hopefully, safety. He turned away, jammed both saddle pistols in his belt, hung the quiver of arrows at his side, and quickly strung the Mongol bow. With rifle in one hand and the bow in the other, he started up the back side of the rimrock to his chosen place. The bald granite knob reminded him of a Jesuit friar with his bald head and hair that hung over his ears. The grey downed timber lay like so many feathered arrows pointing downhill, but the promontory on the bald knob held enough scrub oak brush for cover. He positioned his weapons with the intent of giving the impression of many men lying in ambush for the coming war party. He would have to move quickly and reload rapidly if he wanted to stop them. Once everything was positioned, he sat down, leaning back against a large chunk of granite, and watched the trail below. While he watched, he used a small piece of charcoal to draw a message on the yellow ribbon. With figures similar to those of the petroglyphs, he drew figures that told if they continued, many would die, if they turned around they would live. He grinned and tied it to one of his whistlers.

His scope lay in his lap as he watched the trail where it came from the trees into the small meadows. One man rode well out front, a scout, following the exact trail of Gabe and company. They had made no effort to try to hide their passing, preferring to cover more ground and hopefully escape without a confrontation, but the Blackfoot were determined. The scout reined up, looking up at the long line of rimrock, shading his eyes as he searched the saddle with the pass. Gabe was relieved to know they had already crossed over and the others were well on their way to safety, but as he thought of safety, he saw the rest of the raiding party come from the trees. He counted as they came into the valley and they numbered eighteen. More than he expected, even though he saw the group earlier, apparently some had not caught up with the rest of the band. He breathed deep, shaking his head and muttering a quick prayer, finishing with, "Lord, I need all the help I can get!"

He nocked the yellow ribbon arrow and stood as he brought the bow to full draw. He looked below, judging the distance to the meadow about three hundred yards, and let the arrow fly. It arced high overhead, screaming like a terrified nighthawk and trailing the ribbon. He dropped to one knee, snatched up his scope and watched the warriors. Instantly every head looked skyward, caught the image of the arrow as it sounded the shrill cry as it descended. Horses became skittish, sidestepping, warriors grew wide-eyed, watching the arrow descend and impale itself no more than ten feet in front of the leaders. The men looked at one another, at the arrow, and began searching the trees for the archer. A wave of a hand from the leader and a warrior jumped to the ground and retrieved the arrow and handed it up to the war leader. Gabe watched all the while with his scope, saw the man stretch out the ribbon and look at the pictograph message then lift his eyes to the rimrock.

Gabe stood, waving his arms and shouted, "I am Spirit Bear! Do not follow or you will die!" He heard his words echo from the granite walls on the far side of the lower ravine, and was sure the warriors had heard, but there was no way of knowing if they understood.

There was no response and Gabe sent another arrow, but lifted his sight so the arrow would fall in the midst of the band of warriors. A sudden scream told Gabe his arrow had found its mark, striking one of the warriors, but no one fell, although the rest scattered into the trees. He knew it was a startling revelation to anyone, especially to those who were skilled with bows and arrows, to see someone able to send an arrow many times the distance they thought an arrow could fly. They would need time to decide what to do, and he was willing to give them plenty of time, hopefully to choose to stop their pursuit, but he also would have to wait to see just what they thought was the best course of action.

12 / Blackfoot

Gabe glanced left and right, mentally positioning himself for his defense, then lifted the scope for a closer look at the band of Blackfoot warriors, barely visible in the tree line below. He scanned the entire line of trees that hung in the shadows of the taller mountain behind him, watching for any movement that would be a giveaway of their tactics and maybe offer a target. He saw several warriors standing beside their horses, but the obvious leader was still mounted as he directed his men. Well, guess that's it then. They're gonna try to charge, so . . . He breathed deep, stood and nocked another arrow. He saw a break in the trees that offered a sight on one of the leaders that still sat his horse and he judged the distance at just over three hundred yards. Although he had hit targets at greater distances, the many variables, height, wind, tree branches, and more, made it uncertain. But he wanted to let the Blackfoot they were still vulnerable, and he let the arrow fly.

He dropped to one knee as he watched the feathered missile arc and begin its descent. It whispered through the thin mountain air and pierced the man's arm, pushed through and buried itself in the side of the leader, who tumbled from his horse, startling the other warriors. He heard shouts and war cries as he watched the men move further into the trees. Suddenly the trees spilled warriors, screaming and charging horseback, filling the small meadow. Gabe grabbed his rifle, brought it to bear on one of the warriors leading the charge and fired. The Ferguson spat its lead and fire and the warrior's chest blossomed red as he was upended to roll off the rump of his mount.

Before the first man fell, Gabe was on the run to the next placement of his weapons. He grabbed up the saddle pistol. The .52 caliber thirteen-inch barrel gave the weapon accuracy that rivaled a long rifle, and he drew bead on another warrior, dropped the hammer and sent him on his way to the other side. He took several steps to his right, cocking the hammer for the lower barrel and took aim at a third man. He fired, and saw the target slump, but not fall. Gabe was already on his way back past his first perch, and snatched up the second pistol, and chose another rider, close to the lead, and fired, but his aim was low, and the horse stumbled, throwing his rider over his head. Gabe cocked the second hammer as he moved further to his left, chose a target, and fired, scoring another hit. He dropped the big pistol and ran back to his original position.

His goal had been to give the Blackfoot the impression there were many shooters atop the ridge and that they faced a formidable force. He grabbed up the Ferguson, quickly reloaded and chose another target. The charge was nearing the trees below the ridge, but he scored another hit, dropping a warrior from his mount into a pile of rocks at the foot of the slope. He searched for another target as he quickly reloaded, he was spinning the trigger guard up to close the breech when a growl came from behind him. He twisted around to see Wolf, teeth bared, and hackles raised, but looking to a cut in the rocks. A warrior was rising from the cut, drawing an arrow, as Gabe rolled to the side, pulling his belt pistol and cocking it as he rolled. From his belly flop position he fired the pistol, obscuring his target with the grey cloud of smoke, but he heard the bullet strike flesh and the warrior cry out.

As Gabe rose, he was rotating the barrels on his belt pistol, and cocking the second hammer, but the warrior was gone, having tumbled backwards off the rimrock and crashed to the rocks below. Gabe reached down and stroked the neck of the wolf as he searched for any other warriors trying to mount the rimrock. "Thanks boy. I thought I told you to take care of the women, but I reckon she figgered you'd be more help to me. Glad she did!" He glanced at the rimrock, knowing he had underestimated the Blackfoot. He was certain none could climb the precipice, but one had and if one could, perhaps there would be more.

He visually reviewed his position, remembering there were two ways anyone could approach his promontory. One was the way chosen by the now dead warrior, the other was the thin line of trees beside the steep trail near the slide rock. The second line was far to his right, but it would difficult at best, but not impossible, for anyone to reach those trees without coming under his fire. He moved from position to position, reloading his weapons and watching below. He guessed the Blackfoot were regrouping before assaulting the open trail below his perch that would expose them to his fire.

They did not wait but a few moments and two men were sacrificed for the others to see if and when or where their assailant or assailants would reveal themselves. They were certain they would have an opportunity to return fire if that happened. But they were disappointed, for Gabe was well positioned and back from the edge of the rimrock, totally unseen from below. The trail was so steep, that the horses, though driven hard by their riders, could only hump and lunge as they assaulted the slope, giving Gabe ample time to take them both with arrows. He watched as they fell, and the horses, stopped and turned back to retreat into the trees.

Gabe moved to his right, closer to the trail that crested the saddle of the pass, always watching the trail below. The clatter of hooves warned him that more were coming. He dropped to one knee, lifted the saddle pistol, steadying it with his left hand, elbow resting on his knee. He brought it to bear on the first man, dropped the hammer and squinted through the smoke to see him drop his lance and grab his chest with one hand, twist the mane in his other hand, and slap legs to the horse, urging him up the slope. Gabe aimed for the second man, fired, and scored a hit, and watched the man slump over the side of his horse, who stopped and craned his neck around to see his rider on the ground. The big paint horse stepped back, turned and sauntered into the trees, leaving the dead rider where he fell.

The first rider, though wounded, had made it to the trees but Gabe knew that part of the trail would require him to climb through the slide rock and lead his horse, but surely he would not succeed at that with a half-inch ball of lead in his chest. Gabe quickly reloaded the pistol, lay it on the rock, and returned to his rifle. He saw the head and neck of a horse, but the rider was obscured by the branches of a spruce tree, yet visible. Gabe brought the front blade sight between the buckhorns of the rear sight and squeezed off his shot. The sound of the big .62 caliber ball striking flesh was distinct, and the cry of the target assured Gabe he had scored a hit as the figure disappeared on the far side of his horse.

Gabe instantly reloaded, watching the trail, but no one showed. He breathed deep, hoping it was finished. Most warrior bands are leery of taking too many losses and would choose to leave rather than suffer more casualties, but these were Blackfoot, known to be the fiercest warriors in the north and feared by most of the other tribes. Gabe shook his head, waiting, tired of killing. He hadn't kept count, but he guessed there were at least a half-dozen dead and that was about a third of their fighting force. Most leaders would have withdrawn long before this, but this man, this Buffalo Bull's Back Fat, must be trying to build a reputation as a fierce warrior, but he was doing it at the expense of his warriors.

As Gabe contemplated, he saw movement in the trees. Then a voice was raised, the language was French, probably learned from some of the Hudson's Bay traders. "We will leave! You are too many, and we have lost many warriors. We will leave!"

Gabe responded in a shout, "I am Spirit Bear. Your warriors have fought and died bravely. Take

your dead, I will not shoot. We will fight no more!"
He stayed at his place, refusing to expose himself
in case this was a trap of some sort, and he waited.
Four warriors, all afoot, held close to the trees and
the rocks of the rimrock as they approached the
downed warriors. Three lay by the trail below, one
was brought draped across his horse from the upper
end of the trail by the slide rock.

When he saw the band break into the lower
meadow, Gabe watched with his scope, counting both
warriors and horses with bodies, and was satisfied
the entire band had left. He breathed deep, slowly
stood and went to retrieve his other weapons. Ebony
bobbed his head at the approach of his man and
whinnied softly. Gabe slipped the loaded weapons in
the holsters and scabbard, hung the quiver of arrows
by the cantle and slid the cased and unstrung bow
beneath the left saddle fender. He mounted up and
started on the trail to rejoin his friends, tired, but
relieved.

13 / Rest

Gabe shrugged into his wool capote, made from a five-point Hudson's Bay blanket, letting the hood hang on his shoulders. The dun colored blanket had colorful stripes across the bottom that covered his legs to his knees. The tall peaks that surrounded him still held deep snow in the crevices and crevasses, the bald tops mostly blown free by the high-altitude winds. The thick black timber sported patches of white drifts that would be held until deeper into the summer when the hot sun could penetrate the dark shadows. Wolf trotted before Ebony, often scampering off the trail to sniff and explore, but before long, he was found sitting, tongue lolling, showing he was tired and wanted a ride.

Gabe stepped down and lifted the furball, laying him belly down across his bedroll behind the cantle of his saddle, causing Ebony to be a little skittish, but he knew the wolf and held pretty steady. Gabe stepped aboard, checked his backtrail for any pursuit and pointed the big black down the trail. The trickle of a stream that carried some late spring runoff from higher up was soon a real creek, splashing and chattering its way through the narrow ravine. The smaller creek was joined by two others that found their way through narrow gorges and added their flow to make the stream more of a challenge to follow as it bullied its way between the broad-shouldered mountains. Steep timbered hillsides, solid granite cliffs, and random talus slopes crowded one another, challenging each other for toeholds in the narrow valley that lay innocently between the intimidating mountains.

Gabe watched for signs of a camp where he would find his friends, but no smoke showed, and their tracks continued to show the animals were running. He was glad to see they had heeded his advice and made a quick getaway from the threat of the Blackfoot, but now he wondered just how far they had traveled. He guessed he had covered about four or five miles since the pass, and as he rounded a low alluvial plane, he broke into a wide valley that stretched green and lush before him. The river meandered its way through the valley floor, picking up additional waters from other runoff streams that cascaded from the high mountains and the snow that struggled to stay longer.

The mouth of the valley was pinched to a narrow passage by a massive alluvial plane and talus slope probably formed eons ago with rockslides and avalanches as the wide and deep formation pushed into the valley. The sun was dropping behind the high mountains and the deep shadows covered the west facing crags, slowly working their way up the west slopes. He reined up and looked at the unusual formations, guessing this would be a good place for an ambush and thought this might be where he found his friends. That thought had no sooner filled his mind than he heard the challenge come from the rocks, "You look like Gabe, and that horse is his, but if you ain't, you better high tail it outta here 'fore I decide to shoot!"

Gabe grinned, recognizing the voice of Ezra, lifted his hands over his head and answered in a somewhat girlish voice, "Oh, massa, please don't shoot! I been duckin' arrows and bullets an' such all day, and I'm plumb tuckered out!"

Ezra started down from the rocks, rifle at his side as he picked his footing among the loose stones. He looked at Gabe, "Take much to convince 'em to quit followin' us?"

"Too much. But I had a good spot and they thought there was more than just me, so, they chose to leave, and I was mighty glad of it," explained Gabe as he gigged Ebony to a walk beside Ezra.

"Camp's up thataway. Women should have dinner ready," explained Ezra, then looking at the wolf, "Otter'll be glad to see you and him too! She told him to go back to you and he took off, but she wasn't sure what he'd do."

"He saved my bacon is what he did," added Gabe, reaching back to stroke Wolf's scruff.

"I think the women are plannin' on taking a few days here. They wanna get them wolf pelts finished and I don't know what all."

"Hey, a few days sittin' around sounds fine with me."

The women were fashioning stretch frames for the three wolf pelts they took after the wolf pack attack. The others were mangy and mauled and were left behind. Otter looked up when Wolf came bouncing into camp, then when she saw Gabe, both women jumped to their feet to greet their men. Otter hung on Gabe's neck, looking deep into his eyes, and said, "I knew your God would bring you back to me."

Gabe smiled, held her close, and said, "Yeah, about that. We're gonna have to have a nice long talk about God. You need to get to know Him better."

"I would like that."

He drew her closer, kissed her and leaned back to look at her. "You sure are pretty, you know that?"

Otter smiled, "You keep telling me that, so it must be so!"

"All right you two! I'm so hungry my belly button's pinchin' my backbone! How 'bout gettin' supper goin'?" rasped Ezra, still holding Dove close. He looked down at Dove, grinning as she playfully slapped his arm, smiling up at him.

Their camp lay at the edge of the trees that populated a small peninsula that pushed the Shoshone River around its point. While the stand of timber on the peninsula was small, no more than fifty or sixty yards wide at any point, the basin was nearer two hundred yards wide and close to three hundred yards long. A small pond lay on the far side of the river, but grass was plentiful. As Gabe stretched out, using his saddle for a pillow, he looked up the talus slope to a rocky crag that formed a knob, while behind the knob rose snowcapped mountain peaks. The slopes on both sides of the river were littered with grey skeletons of long downed trees, all lying perfectly parallel with tops pointing downhill. He asked Otter, "What caused those trees to be like that?"

Otter looked up from her tending the meat frying in the skillet, then at Gabe, "Avalanche," came the simple answer.

"You mean the snow piled up that high and came down and wiped out all those trees?"

"Yes, it does that in these high mountains. Nothing can stop it," she answered, unconcerned.

Gabe shook his head, muttered, "Amazing," and continued his survey of the mountain valley. As an afterthought, he turned to Ezra as he rose, "I'm gonna take my scope and climb up there a little ways, do a check of our back trail, just to be sure."

Ezra was too comfortable and dozy to do more than grunt an acknowledgment as Gabe started his climb. Gabe had no more than seated himself, when he felt the Wolf rub up against his leg wanting some attention. Gabe rubbed his scruff behind his ears and drew the animal close, then lifted the scope to look back up the valley. Once he was satisfied there was no one on their trail, he began to scan the mountain slopes on both sides of the valley. He saw movement high up and focused the scope to see five mountain goats, white hair camouflaging them among the patches of snow, small black horns, hooves, and noses the only distinguishing color to mark their presence.

A big billy goat stood on a precarious ledge above the others, watching the antics of the nannies and kids as they played and grazed on the high-country tidbits that flowered in the tundra. Gabe lowered his scope, saw the tiny figures high up, then lifted the scope for a wider scan. Lower down and on the opposite side, he saw a lone bighorn sheep, sitting in the remaining bit of direct sun, chewing his cud and dozing. With another slow scan, he was satisfied and stood to start his return to the camp. Wolf jumped off the rock and seemed to bounce from rock to rock as he made his descent and Gabe followed.

At the campfire, Otter started dishing up the food, and asked Gabe, "How long will we stay here?"

"Oh, couple days or so, if you want. Will that be enough time to finish those?" he asked, pointing to the wolf pelts with his chin, reaching for the offered tin plate.

Otter smiled, glanced at Dove, nodded, and looked back at Gabe. "Yes, we can finish those in two days, maybe three."

Gabe looked at Ezra who nodded his agreement, and answered, "Good, we'll just rest up a mite and I'm sure the horses won't mind either." He sat on a small boulder and started eating. Otter joined him, handed him a cup of camp coffee, which was a blend of coffee and chicory, and smiled as she leaned her head on his shoulder. They were happy together.

14 / Deviation

When the men returned from their early morning times with the Lord, their meal was simmering on the big flat rock beside the low-burning fire. The coffee pot sat close to the embers and the smells of venison and turnip stew lingered. While the women worked the pelts, the men sat and enjoyed their morning repast, occasionally glancing toward the women and their labor with the pelts. Gabe set the tin plate aside, poured his coffee and rose to go to the worksite of the women. They were on their knees as they leaned over the wolf hides that were stretched and tied onto large hoops made from alder branches bound together.

Gabe leaned against the trunk of a spruce as he watched the women applying a pink colored slurry to the hides, using the shoulder blade of a recently taken elk to both stretch the hide and rub the slurry deep into the pores. He knew the slurry was made of brains and water and would soften and cure the hides into a soft leather. He had watched this process before when he and Ezra had found Singing Bird and Badger Tail, two Shoshone youngsters who had been left behind because of the Smallpox plague that struck the band while on a buffalo hunt. Singing Bird had tanned some deer hides to make clothes for her and her brother while Gabe and Ezra helped, learning much about the process.

"Sure am glad I had my breakfast 'fore I watched that!" declared Gabe, somewhat amazed at the skill of Otter and Dove and their willingness to use the brain slurry and rub it into the hide with their hands. Both had slurry on their hands, arms, and even a spot or two on their faces when they obviously had to scratch an itch. He grinned as Otter turned to look at him and said, "You could always join us down here and help."

"Nope. Your father, Black Bear, told me that is woman's work!" he answered, grinning.

Otter sat back on her heels, scowling at her man. "Black Bear is my mother. My father is Red Pipe!" She knew Gabe knew the proper names, but he had spoken before of Black Bear as the head of their family because of her strong manner. Her father most often yielded to her demands and allowed her to take the lead in many things.

"Oh, that's right! I keep forgetting!" replied Gabe, exaggerating his motions of regret, slapping his leg as if he just remembered. Otter picked up a handful of slurry and cocked her arm back as if to throw it at Gabe, but he ducked and ran back to the fire, out of range of her throw and annoyance.

The women soon finished with the slurry and stretching of the hides and lay them in the sun to dry. After an overnight drying, they would stretch the hides again, then smoke them, a step that would aid in the softening and help the leather to be water resistant. They washed up, and walked to the fire for some coffee, a habit established by a winter with the men and their need for coffee.

Once seated beside their men, holding the warm cups with both hands, enjoying the rising fragrance, Otter looked at Gabe and said, "Tell me."

"Tell you? Tell you what?"

"More about your God. You said you would tell us," stated Otter.

Gabe glanced at Ezra, wanting to yield to his greater experience in spiritual matters since he was the son of a pastor, but Ezra just gave a slight nod for Gabe to take the lead. He looked at Otter and began, "Well, you've told me that your people refer to the Great Spirit as Tam Apo or Our Father. And that when you die it is like a journey or pilgrimage to the land beyond the setting sun and when one dies you leave things like weapons and more, even kill horses to join the dead to make that journey. But you never know for certain what happens. Is that right?"

Otter dropped her eyes, then looked back at Gabe, a somber expression painting her face, "Yes. That has always bothered me. That all seems to be for the warriors and if they have fought well and earned honors, then there is another life for them. But nothing for the women. And we cannot know for sure," answered Otter, quietly.

"And I've heard some refer to the Sun God, the spirits of earth, wind, fire, sky, and more. Even the spirit animals, like the wolf and coyote, isn't that right?" asked Gabe.

"Yes, our elders taught those things," replied Otter, glancing to Dove who nodded her agreement.

"Well, God is not like those you have known. He wants everyone to know how to get to Heaven and made the way simple so warrior, women, children, everyone could go when they die. But He also tells us it's not something we have to earn. He says, *'For by grace are ye saved through faith; and that not of yourselves: it is the gift of God: not of works, lest any man should boast.'* He says it isn't because of the things we do, like being a great warrior or anything else. It is a gift, but like any gift, it is a gift that has to be received."

"But, how do we receive that gift?" implored

Otter, glancing to Dove and Ezra.

Gabe took a deep breath, flipped some pages in the Bible and began, "Four things we need to know, the first is told here," and he pointed to the verse in Romans 3:23 and read, " *'For all have sinned and come short of the glory of God.'* That says that all of us have done wrong, or done some bad things, and because of that, we come short or don't quite make it to Heaven. For example, I know there have been times I did wrong, said something that wasn't true, took something that wasn't mine, you know, those things we all do that we shouldn't. You understand that, don't you?" Otter hung her head, remembering something from her past, and nodded as she lifted her eyes to Gabe.

"Well, there's more. Over here," again pointing to the scriptures, Romans 6:23, "It says, *'For the wages of sin is death;'* So, because we've done those bad things, what we deserve is death. Now, that's not just dying, that means dying and going to Hell forever. That's a horrible place of fire and worse." He looked at Otter, saw her brow wrinkle as she listened, then he continued, "But the rest of this verse talks about that gift we mentioned, *'but the gift of God is eternal life through Jesus Christ our Lord.'"* He smiled as he looked at Otter whose frown turned into a smile as well.

"That's the second thing, knowing that there is a

penalty for our sin. But the third thing is to know that God offers us the gift of eternal life. That's life forever in Heaven! Now the fourth thing is to know how to receive that gift and that is told here in these verses," he pointed to Romans 10:9, *"That if thou shalt confess with thy mouth the Lord Jesus, and shalt believe in thine heart that God hath raised him from the dead, thou shalt be saved. (v.13) For whosoever shall call upon the name of the Lord shall be saved.'* That fourth thing is to believe in your heart and call upon the Lord. We do that in prayer. Do you understand?" he looked at Otter who had scooted forward on her seat, drawing closer to Gabe as she looked expectantly into his eyes. He smiled, glanced at Dove and saw her nodding to Ezra, then back at Otter.

"So, if we pray and ask for that gift, He will give it to us? That gift of, what's it called? Eternal life? That means if we ask for it, He will give it to us, and we'll live forever in Heaven?" pleaded Otter as she leaned toward Gabe.

"That's right."

"How do we pray?" she asked.

"Well, I'll start us off, and you listen and as you believe in your heart, you can pray in the same way." Gabe lowered and closed his eyes as he reached for Otter's hand and began to pray. It was a simple prayer to thank God for all He had done for them, to thank

Him for providing the Savior, Jesus Christ, and for the gift of eternal life. As he continued, he said, "Now, Otter, Dove, if you believe with all your heart, then just pray and say something like, 'Forgive me for my sins, and I accept your gift of eternal life to live with You in heaven forever, make it real in my life and help me to walk in your ways. Amen.'" He listened as each one prayed in her own words and asked forgiveness and to receive the gift of salvation. When they finished with an Amen, he drew Otter close and embraced her, and looked over her shoulder to see Ezra and Dove embracing as well.

Otter daubed at her tears, then pointed to the Bible and asked, "Will you teach me these signs so I may learn more about God?"

Gabe chuckled, "Of course. But it might take a while."

"Then we should start now!" she declared, much to the delight of Gabe. He chuckled, drew her close and said, "We'll do it."

15 / Journey

It was a well-used game trail, probably traveled most often by migrating herds of elk and was well beaten down as it picked its way through the fallen timbers and rocky soil of the talus slope. It was slow going but offered ample opportunity for the riders to get a close up of the unimaginable terrain of the high-country. The riders were dwarfed by the mountains that stood as pillars of heaven itself. The granite tipped peaks held the glaciers and snowpack tightly to their bosoms, letting the relentless sun of early summer milk the icy fields of runoff water so needed by the lower valleys and plains. Cool breezes whispered from high above to push the horses, tails to the wind, down the shadowy canyon.

Once off the talus, the riders found themselves on an easier trail that followed the grassy flats of the bottom of the gorge but were separated from the river by a basaltic formation that blackened the flat with its volcanic detritus from some ancient eruption in the mountains. But they soon broke into a brushy valley bottom that pushed the trail to the west side of the river and rode the shoulder at the foot of the mountains. The trail was narrow and the going still relatively easy, so Gabe chose to push on without a mid-day break. The horses were taking it easy and picking their footing, as the trail slowly descended from the high-country.

Just after mid-day, the mountains pushed in, narrowing the gorge and the riders were forced to cross the icy stream to take to a trail that hung on the east slope. At the edge of the stream and before they climbed unto the trail, Gabe stepped down, "Maybe we need to rest 'em up a little while, don't want 'em gettin' lazy on that trail. It looks a little precarious."

"What we can see of it don't look too bad, but when it disappears round that knob yonder, I just don't know. You don't suppose it ends down there somewhere and leaves us hangin' on the side of a cliff with no place to turn around?" asked Ezra.

"You could have gone all day and not say somethin' like that!" declared Gabe, shaking his head. "But I don't see any other way out of these mountains, do you?"

"Uhnuhn, nope, sure don't. Guess we'll just hafta give it a go!" answered Ezra.

The start of the trail on the east slope was across a swath of slide rock where any misstep would result in a nasty fall on the sharp-edged stones. Each stone was flat and wide granite, none more than two feet across, marked by green and orange moss that added to the slippery surface. Every rock balanced on the one below it, teeter-totter fashion, none offering solid footing. It was only the blown in dirt that accumulated on the time worn trail that gave any semblance of footing for the horses. Cloven-hoofed elk, deer, and mountain sheep were not challenged by the crossing, but mountain savvy horses were constantly wary.

Once the trail rounded the knob mentioned by Ezra, it had risen about four hundred feet above the river in the bottom of the gorge and moved into a brushy shoulder that gave a sense of reprieve or safety. But that feeling was soon dissipated when they broke from the scrub oak and encountered another rock slide, although not as wide as the first, but then it became a narrow shelf that hung high above the river that was visible only by looking almost straight down past their stirrups, to see the white water of the river below. Ebony carefully picked his footing on the narrow trail, occasionally bending his neck to peer over the edge, then leaning into the sheer wall. Across the canyon, another stream cascaded down a steep mountainside, waterfall after waterfall crashing white water over the rocks, the roar of the cascades echoing off the canyon walls.

They rounded another heavily timbered shoulder, a small slide, and then the trail twisted its way to the canyon bottom as the gorge widened to accompany three more feeder creeks. They crossed the river to the west side and took the trail that rode the low shoulder, then another crossing, a mountain hugging trail and suddenly the mouth of the canyon bid them welcome. Gabe reined up for a long look as Otter and the others came alongside. "Whoooeee, that's a mighty welcome sight!" he declared, nodding to the widening valley and the distant flats.

"If we'd had to cross any more rockslides, I was ready to sit on one o' them rocks and just wait for the Lord to come get me!" proclaimed Ezra, leaning forward on the pommel, stretching his legs.

Otter stood in her stirrups, pointed to the river bottom, "There, across the river where that small mound is, would be a good camp."

Gabe looked where she pointed, grinned. "Looks good to me, let's go!"

They spent one night at the chosen camp, but were anxious to move further down the valley, needing some fresh meat and hoping for a buffalo. They moved out early, as the eastern horizon shaded from pink to grey to muted blue. It was a cloudless day and the promised warmth was a welcome change from the cold air and shaded valleys of the mountains. They rode side by side, following the meandering river, crossing the occasional feeder creek, and watching for game sign. It promised to be a good day.

***

Jacques Beauchamp and Charles Ducette rode side by side, both trailing loaded packhorses. Their foray along the Yellowstone river and its southerly fork had been a profitable choice. Leaving a trail of dead bodies, ravaged women, and burnt lodges, the raiders had amassed considerable goods now carried by twelve horses stolen from two villages of Crow. Ducette commented, "Like you figgered, ain't gonna hafta split the goods like we first thought. What with them two 'mericans and that Miniconjou gettin' kilt." He chuckled, twisted in his saddle to look behind at the others, then turned back and spoke a little lower, "Course, we could lose a few more'n I wouldn't complain."

"I don't wanna lose any till we get back to the Missouri River. We got a couple weeks to go, and a lotta country to cover. Probably find some more villages and easy pickin's and we need them to take them villages or whatever we come acrost," answered Beauchamp, scratching at his bushy beard.

He picked out a hardback, cracked it between his fingernails and tossed it aside. "Sure don't wanna lose that Mandan. He's put us onto some good raids, and we need him to get us back to the big river."

"Think we'll be buildin' rafts to take this stuff downriver?" asked Ducette.

"Yeah, I'm thinkin' that's gonna be the easiest. An' if we lose some more men, it'll be easier to take rafts than handle all these horses."

"There might be another way," said Peter Marchand, who had been riding behind the two and overheard their conversation. He moved his horse alongside the two, "That big guy," nodding to those behind, "Beaulieux. I was talkin' to him the other night 'fore we turned in, and he was a boatmaker for the Northwest Company. He said he made several big bateaux to haul their trade goods upriver and the pelts downriver. He said with a little help, it'd be just as easy to make them as a raft and they'd be much more manageable."

Beauchamp grinned, glanced at Ducette, "That sounds even better. Even if it took a day or two more, it'd be better travelin' downriver in one o' them instead of standin' on a raft!"

Ducette chuckled, "The size of him, I wouldn't have thought he could do anything but fight."

"We'll talk more about it after we set up camp for the night. I wanna see just how much he knows about boatbuilding and such. Maybe we won't hafta wait till we get to the Missouri 'fore we take to the water," commented Beauchamp, cocking his head to the side as he considered the new development and the possibilities afforded.

16 / Resupply

Gabe and company made camp in the shadow of a saddleback mountain that marked the eastern end of the Absaroka mountain range. Between their camp and the lone timber covered mountain, a ridge of a series of humpback hills, striped with dull red and off-white streaks, made Gabe think the Creator had used a hopping jackrabbit to form the hills. He chuckled to himself as he pictured a giant jackrabbit hopping about unhindered and uncontrolled. The sun was low in the western sky, seeming to rest atop the jagged mountain horizon. Long lances of gold shot across the sky and the brilliance of the setting sun glared in defiance as another day came to a colorful end.

They were beside a small creek that fed the Shoshone river just below the larger confluence of the north and south forks of the greater stream. Tall cottonwoods with scattered aspen gave cover and shade and the grassy flat offered knee-deep graze for the animals. Gabe gave each a long tether, while Ezra stacked their gear near the trees. The women were busying themselves with the fire and preparations for the meal when Gabe returned, "I'm gonna go have a look around from that hill yonder. Prob'ly won't go clear to the top, but I wanna get a better idea where we are and such."

Otter was used to her man and his continual surveying of the nearby country and was content with his efforts for knowledge and preparations for their safety. She felt secure and content with her man and smiled as he walked from the camp, his broad shoulders stretching the buckskin tunic she made for him, the fringe swishing side to side with his long strides. His long dark blonde hair covered the collar and even from where she sat, she saw the whiskers of his beard. She was proud of her man and happy with him. She glanced at Dove who was watching her as her eyes followed Gabe, saw her grinning and laughed. They both knew what the other thought and as sisters, shared similar feelings for their men.

When Gabe returned, the meal was ready and they enjoyed the time together as they ate the broiled venison strip steaks, roasted timpsila and camas bulbs, and cornmeal biscuits. Gabe took a long sip of the hot brew and sat back, "You know, I'm gettin' so used to the chicory, I don't know if I could ever get used to plain coffee again!"

Ezra chuckled, "Oh, it's good alright, but give me pure hot coffee any day!"

"Will you go hunt tomorrow?" asked Otter, looking to Gabe and Ezra.

"Yeah, I know we're gettin' low on meat, and while I was up on that mountain behind us, I saw a bunch of elk upstream on this little creek. There was ample brush and grass for 'em so I think they'll bed down there and make for good huntin' in the mornin'," answered Gabe.

"Well, while you go after them elk, I think I'm gonna check out that other stream yonder and see if I can catch us a batch o' fish. I've been hankerin' for some trout!" added Ezra, finishing up his plate of food by wiping up the remains with his biscuit.

"While you two do that, we," pointing with her chin to her sister, "will start making smoking racks for the meat. But first, we have a surprise for you!"

"A surprise? What kind of surprise?" asked Gabe, seeing Ezra frown at the suggestion of a surprise.

"You'll see," she answered, standing and going to the packs. She gathered up fresh buckskins and blankets, aided by Dove, and the two grinned as Otter said, "Follow us."

Gabe looked at Ezra, grinned, "Since they got clothes and blankets, I'm thinkin' their plannin' on a bath!"

Ezra feigned alarm, shrugging his shoulders as he answered, "Bath!? We don't need no bath, why, we took one just last summer!" Both men laughed as they rose to follow the women knowing 'last summer' was not more than two weeks past when they bathed before crossing the mountain pass.

As they rounded the shoulder of the mountain, the men were surprised to see steam rising from an aqua colored pool that emptied into a small stream that led to the river. They frowned at the sight, looked at the women to see them grinning and setting the bundles on the rocks nearby. Otter said, "This is where we will wash. It is nice and warm because of the hot springs there," nodding her head at the trickle of water bubbling up from a white and orange mound set against the slope of the mountain, sheltered by a cluster of piñon. "It is too hot when it comes from the ground, but is nice and warm here," added Otter, as she removed her moccasins and started to the water, still attired in her tunic and leggings.

"Aren't you gonna take off your buckskins?" asked Gabe, frowning.

"No, they need to be washed also, come on!" she motioned to Gabe as she disappeared into the cloud of steam that rose into the dusk, but the buckskins soon came flying out of the cloud amidst the giggles of the pair.

Ezra looked at Dove, "Guess they'll tell us when it's

our turn," and glanced back at the pool and steam cloud. It wasn't a modesty issue, but a practical one, that kept both couples from the water. Always concerned for safety, one couple stood by with rifles in hand, watching the hillside that was now shadowed in the deepening darkness of dusk, and the valley beyond for any sign of danger. When Gabe and Otter finished, they would stand guard for Ezra and Dove. Wolf dozed nearby, chin resting between his paws, one eyebrow lifting and eye opening just a slit at any movement, then dozing again, his lip quivering with each breath.

A long arm reached for a blanket at the edge of the pool and soon two blanket clad figures emerged from the steam cloud, laughing. Gabe looked at Ezra, "Your turn!" and turned back to Otter as they walked to the rock that held the clean buckskins. The wet set would be dried by the fire, absorbing some of the smoke to aid in keeping the leather soft, but they would still require some stretching and working as they dried. Ezra and Dove soon emerged, dressed, and the four started back to camp, Wolf trailing lazily behind, all were happy and refreshed with their experience in the hot springs. But unseen and unknown by the couples, another set of eyes followed them from the pool to their camp near the trees.

***

"There are four. Two women, two men. One man is like the buffalo," declared Crow's Heart, the Mandan scout for the raiders. He pointed at his hair and the skin on his arm as he described the second man.

Beauchamp scowled, "The buffalo?"

"The buffalo. Hair like buffalo, skin dark like buffalo."

Beauchamp looked at Ducette, "He must mean a negra, prob'ly escaped slave! Why, he'd be worth more'n a whole packhorse o' pelts!"

Ducette looked at Crow's Heart, "The women, are they white?"

"No, native, Crow mebbe. Good lookin' women," he grinned at the remembered image of the women coming from the hot springs.

"We ain't takin' any wimmen," declared Beauchamp.

Ducette grinned, "If we take the negra and sell him, we could take the women and sell them too! An' if they can speak English, they'd be worth as much as the negra!"

Beauchamp's scowl lessened as he looked at Ducette, "All right, but only if they speak English. Most times, women're more trouble than they're worth! Especially 'round this bunch!" he growled, nodding toward the men at the other fire.

Beauchamp looked at Crow's Heart, "Think they'll still be there in the mornin'?"

"Yes. Women make smoke racks for meat. Be there one, two days, mebbe," answered the Mandan, nodding.

"They got anything besides the women?" asked Ducette.

"Uhnn," grunted the Mandan. "Two pack horses, loaded. Some furs and more. All have rifles, pistols, more."

"How far?" asked Beauchamp.

"One hand, mebbe two," said Crow's Heart. One hand meant the time it took the sun to move the width of four fingers across the sky, or one hour.

"Then come mornin', you head out first thing, we'll follow. I wanna know where they are and what they're doin' 'fore we hit 'em. Those men'll have rifles, maybe pistols. Not like the Crow we've hit. So, we'll have to plan it out when we're closer," instructed Beauchamp.

"Uhhn," grunted Crow's Heart, nodding as he turned away to go to his blankets.

Beauchamp looked at Ducette, "Don't say nuthin' to the others about women! If they're good lookin' and can speak English, I don't want 'em harmed or hurt. They'll be worth too much money to waste on a roll in the hay!"

Ducette was deflated at the order, he had already

envisioned himself with one of the women as his own. But he knew better than to cross Beauchamp, he had seen what the man would do to anyone that went against his orders and no woman was worth dying for, besides, with the fortune they could make on the pelts and slaves, he could have any woman he wanted. He grinned at the thought and turned to his blankets, mumbling to himself.

17 / Raid

Since their talk with the women about the Lord, both couples had begun spending their times with the Lord together. Gabe and Otter climbed the hill behind their camp to the same promontory he used to survey the territory, while Ezra and Dove crossed the creek to a small butte. Otter leaned back against Gabe as they watched the rising sun paint the eastern sky with the colors of early morning. The pinks rose from the horizon and touched the bellies of the few clouds that hung lazily in the morning sky. With the greys pushed aside in favor of muted blue, the sun threw shafts of gold to foretell its rise. "Every sunrise has its own palette of colors," observed Gabe, looking down at Otter as she lifted her face to him. She was seated on the ground, between his knees, elbows on his legs. His forearms rested on her shoulders, his chin touching her head.

Otter smiled at him, twisted around to face him and said, "It is good to be here with you. Our time together with God has been special. I am glad you told me more." She glanced down beside her, reaching out to rumple the scruff on Wolf's neck, then back at Gabe.

He drew her close and they held the embrace for several moments. As they leaned back, Gabe looked below and said, "Looks like those two are going back to camp. Reckon we oughta go have some breakfast 'fore I go after them elk."

Otter smiled, stood up, reached out for Gabe's hands and drew him close as he rose. They kissed and started down the hill, hand in hand, glancing occasionally back at the trailing Wolf and then in Ezra and Dove's direction. Once at camp, the women quickly finished the preparations for breakfast, but Gabe just grabbed a biscuit and piece of meat, "I need to get to that little basin 'fore the elk decide to move out." He glanced at Ezra, "You can eat my share since you're just goin' fishin'!"

Ezra chuckled, "I might have to take that other pack horse to pack them fish back!"

"Ha! There you go, daydreamin' again!" chided Gabe, starting to the horses. He had already geared up Ebony and the sorrel pack horse, knowing if he did down an elk, one horse wouldn't be able to pack it and him back to camp. He kissed Otter, held her close, then turned and mounted up. He waved as he left the camp, pointing Ebony to the flats away from the little stream.

Ezra bided his time in camp, enjoying an extra cup of the chicory blend as he watched the women assemble the rest of the smoke racks in anticipation of fresh elk meat to smoke and dry. He stood, stretched, and with rifle in hand, he drew Dove close with his free arm, kissed her and said, "I'll be back 'fore mid-day, so we'll have fresh trout to cook for our lunch." She smiled at her man, "I'll wait till you return before I stir up the fire." Ezra grinned, shook his head, and walked from camp, bound for the junction of the two rivers and the waiting trout.

Ezra soon found the spot he was looking for, grassy bank, couple of big boulders with backwater pools, easy current and clear water. He cut a long willow, drew his coiled line from his pocket and put a grasshopper he had scooped up as he walked through the grass, on the hook. He stood slightly behind a small cluster of willows and with a couple tries, finally dropped the hook behind the first boulder. Within a few seconds, he felt a tug on the line and jerked back excitedly as he watched a big silvery trout splash from the water, flipping his tail side to side as he fought the hook and suddenly dropped back into the water as the line went slack. Ezra shook his head, pulled the line in by loops that hung from the fingers that held the willow pole, and looked around for another grasshopper. He walked through the grass slowly, seeing a few fluttering away, but carefully moved, determined to find just the right one to catch that big fish.

After following the small feeder creek upstream, when Gabe came to the small meadow, he just caught a glimpse of the pale rumps of the elk herd moving through the trees away from the point of the saddle back mountain. They were moving downstream of a larger creek that probably fed the Shoshone beyond the mountains. But Gabe was determined to get at least one elk and perhaps more and chose to step down to string his bow, preferring the silent kill to the blast of the Ferguson rifle that would give notice to anyone nearby of his presence. He tethered Ebony and the sorrel separately, both loosely tied with a slip knot and well hidden in the trees but with graze nearby and within reach.

The elk had not been spooked and were slowly moving through the thin line of trees, heading toward another small meadow that sat above the slow-moving river less than a mile below. The creek crashed down the rocky ravine, cascading its way to the river below, yet beside the small meadow, it leveled and slowed, offering slow moving water and backwater pools for the animals to take their fill. Gabe worked his way through the timber at the top edge of the meadow, making his way nearer the stream, letting the rushing water mask any noise he might make as he moved.

Two cows and a calf were taking their morning drink, front hooves in the edge of the water, lifting their heads occasionally for a look around. The bigger cow turned away from the stream, snatched a mouthful of grass as she moved away from the water. Gabe was satisfied the younger cow was the mother of the calf and he slowly raised his bow with arrow nocked to take aim at the bigger cow. She lifted her head, looking at the rest of the small herd, took one step and the arrow buried itself to the fletching in her lower chest, just behind the shoulder. The cow stumbled, took two more steps, stumbled and fell to her chest, stretching out her head and neck to try to cushion the fall, but rolled to her side, unmoving. Gabe had nocked another arrow, but the younger cow and calf had turned, jumped and scrambled toward the herd, alerting the others and the entire bunch took off into the trees at the lower end of the small meadow. Within seconds all he saw was the dun colored rumps disappearing into the deep green of the trees.

He stepped out, walked slowly to the downed cow, poked her with his foot, and when she did not respond, he breathed easy and prepared to field dress the animal. He stepped to a rough barked cottonwood, hung his bow and quiver on a stub of a branch and slipped his knife from its scabbard that hung behind his head and between his shoulders. He felt the sharpness, and satisfied, bent to his work.

***

Beauchamp and Ducette led the group as they followed the trail of Crow's Heart. They left the many packhorses and gear back at their camp, anticipating a brief and easy raid on this small number, with a quick return to enjoy their spoils. Crow's Heart was hunkered down behind a rock outcropping high above the camp below and Ducette and Beauchamp were breathing heavy when they came up beside him. Beauchamp nodded for the Mandan scout to explain the situation and he began, "White man leave early, go that way to hunt. Buffalo man there," pointing to the confluence to the two branches of the Shoshone river, "Women in camp."

Beauchamp elbowed his way closer to the edge of the rocks, looking down on the camp and toward the confluence of the rivers. He turned for a steady gaze following the small stream to the distant meadow and looked at Crow's Heart, "I don't see any animals in that meadow."

"Leave early, white man follow."

Beauchamp turned and motioned the others to join them at the promontory. When they came near, he ordered, "Crow's Heart, you take Big Devil and Beaulieux and go after the white man. I don't want any trouble outta him so kill him!" The Mandan looked at the others, nodded to the two biggest men in the entire group, and started back down the slope to their horses. Beauchamp continued, "Marchand," speaking to the Métis, "you take Moreau and Morgan and go after that negra that's up there by the fork," pointing to the confluence of the rivers. "He's prob'ly a runaway slave, but even if he ain't, we're takin' him alive and sellin' him at the slave auction in St. Louis, he'll be worth more'n a half dozen bundles of furs." He glanced at his sidekick, "Ducette, you'n me'll hit the camp where they left the horses, just in case there's anybody guardin' 'em. Then we'll all meet back at that camp down yonder."

Marchand and his two partners nodded and went to the horses as Beauchamp and Ducette took another look at the camp below. Beauchamp counted four horses and a considerable stack of packs and such near the trees, grinning, he turned to Ducette, "This is gonna be easy and very profitable!" They turned away and went to their horses. Their plan was to ride directly into the camp and take the women without a fight. Simple, they thought.

18 / Attack

I'm gonna get that big 'un if it takes me all day!
declared Ezra, barely above a whisper as he talked
to himself. This was his third try, his second cast
had caught a nice pan sized trout, but the big one he
hooked the first time was still lying in the backwater,
lazily pushing against the current and snagging his
dinner from the bugs floating up top. Ezra moved a
little closer, hunkered down so his shadow wouldn't
give warning, then carefully brought back the long
willow pole, and let the cast go, dropping the big
grasshopper just behind the boulder. It dropped
under the ripple, and whirled with the current, then
suddenly the line went taut as the big trout snagged
the bug and ducked away beyond the boulder,
catching the current that took fish, hook, line and
grasshopper. Ezra stepped to the edge of the bank,
willow bent in an arc, line bouncing with the current

and the big fish broke water, splashing into the air, tail whipping side to side. *"Gotchu!"* he mumbled, pulling on the line slowly, bringing the fighting trout closer to the bank. One long leap in the air loosened the line, but Ezra brought it taut and in an instant, the fish flopped up on the bank, bringing Ezra to his knees beside the silvery prize. He put his hand on the fish just behind the gills and started to remove the hook from its jaw.

"Easy now, don't lose him!" came a raspy voice from behind. Ezra twisted around to see two men, both holding cocked rifles trained on him. "Don't do anything we might regret, boy," drawled the Métis.

Ezra glanced to the big boulder where he had lain his rifle and saw a third man sitting on the big rock, grinning at their target. He turned back to the talker, "What do you want?" he asked.

"You. We want you. Where'd you run away from boy?"

"I didn't run away. I'm a freeborn man, I'm from Philadelphia. Anyone there will tell you about me and my family," explained Ezra, starting to rise.

"Don't forget your fish, boy. I think we might like some fish for our dinner!" declared the Métis, Marchand. The other two raiders chuckled, the one on the rock standing, holding Ezra's rifle at his side, his own cradled in his right arm. "Now, you just go easy, keep hold o' them fish, and let's walk back to your camp. He spoke over his shoulder to the others, "Raphael, you fetch our horses and come along. Rene, you come with me as we escort this boy back to his camp."

Beauchamp rode tall in the saddle as he approached the camp. He called out, "Hello the camp! Can I come in? I'm friendly!" He could see through the trees and saw one of the women duck behind the stack of gear, as the other, the shorter of the two, stepped closer to the fire.

"Come in, we've got coffee and biscuits," declared Dove, and she bent to pick up a cup.

Beauchamp had his rifle across the pommel of his saddle, cocked and ready, as he came from the trees. Dove noted the rifle but reached for the coffee pot to pour the man a cup. He swung his leg over the rump of his horse, keeping the rifle clear, even though he had not been invited to step down, which was contrary to the usual accepted manner of the mountains. She started to speak but the man before her leered at her, chuckled and said, "So, two women alone, looks like our lucky day!"

Dove moved her free hand to her back, grasping the handle of her skinning knife, but the man before her cautioned, "Don't do that! I don't wanna hafta kill you. I don't think your man wants you dead, do you?" He glanced toward the stacked gear, saw a rifle muzzle move, then heard Ducette, "Don't do it!"

Otter turned to the new threat, swinging the muzzle of the rifle around, but stopped when she saw a grinning man standing, cocked rifle at his shoulder pointed directly at her. She froze until the man said, "Put it down, nice and easy."

Otter lowered the rifle to rest it on a pair of parfleches, bending at the knees to set it on the containers. She slowly stood, hands held close to her waist, when the man motioned for her to turn around and join her sister. She slowly turned, caught a glimpse of his movement as he lowered the rifle and came behind her. She had yet to take a step and he crowded close, reaching his free arm around her neck. But Otter was prepared, having slipped her knife from the scabbard at her waist, and as he pulled her back against him, she thrust back with the knife, burying it deep in his lower chest. She spun around when he released his grip but held tight to the knife and twisted and cut with it, ripping the blade through his innards.

Ducette's eyes flared, his mouth open as he bent in the middle trying to escape the twisting blade, trying to speak, but a slow whining groan came instead as he slowly slid to the ground and dropped to his face. Otter dropped behind the stack of packs, grabbing her rifle as she did, cocking it and raising it to take a bead on the other man, but his rifle barked and the bullet slammed into the pack in front of her, knocking her off balance. She fell back and tried to rise but the man stood over her, a cocked pistol pointed at her as he growled, "I oughta kill you! That man was my friend!" He slowly shook his head, fighting with himself, wanting vengeance but seeing only the price this woman would bring at a slave market. He breathed deep, motioned for her to get up and join the other woman by the fire as he stepped back, keeping the pistol trained on her. He glanced down at Ducette, and while he looked away, Otter motioned to Wolf to send him after Gabe. Beauchamp glared at the body of his friend, muttering, "You stupid idiot, you just couldn't keep your hands off her!" he growled, then followed Otter to the fire. The wolf had been belly down behind the stack of packs and crawled away unseen.

The big cow was proving to be a challenge for one man. Gabe had split the cow from neck to tail and propped open the rib cage with a stick as he reached into the steaming cavity and pulled the innards out. He pushed the gut pile to the side, knowing the carrion eaters would soon arrive and dispose of the pile. He stood, stretched, pushed at his sleeves to force them up his upper arms and out of the blood that covered him elbow to elbow. He breathed deep, then dropped to one knee beside the big animal, and carefully worked on the hide, peeling it back on one side, then started to stand when he was struck in the back. It was a sudden strike, and he felt it penetrate through his ribs. He didn't think he'd been shot, there had been no gunshot. That must mean it was a knife. He turned to see a big grinning Indian reaching for his tomahawk at his waist, but another man, just as big, dropped the hammer on his rifle and Gabe felt the bullet slam into the side of his head, knocking him backwards and into the water. The current rolled him to his belly and the knife in his back stood like the mast of a sail as the body bobbed in the ripples, painting the water red from his head and the knife in his back. The two men, followed by another walked to the edge of the stream, the current quickening as the slope of the hillside dropped, making the water cascade down and into and over the rocks below. White water, now tinged with blood, carried the inert form with it.

The big man, Rupert Beaulieux was reloading his rifle and withdrew the ramrod from the barrel, reinserting it in the ferrules. He flipped up the frizzen, put powder in the pan and snapped the frizzen down as he lifted the weapon to his shoulder. He held his finger on the rear trigger as he brought the hammer to full cock, then lowered the muzzle to take his sight on the disappearing figure in the water. He slowly lowered the weapon, lining up the sights, took a breath and let some out, then squeezed the thin trigger in the front. The rifle spat flame and smoke from the pan, then the muzzle as it roared and bucked. Yet even from this distance, he saw water splash and the body jerk as he scored another hit.

He lowered his weapon, started the reloading process as he chuckled, "Beauchamp said kill him, so I reckon we done it!"

"We get horses," declared Big Devil, looking at the Mandan. The two men started for the trees to retrieve what they thought would be their own spoils with the horses and the dead man's gear. But when they got to the trees, only the sorrel pack horse was still standing, though somewhat skittish. The big black had jerked free at the first gunshot and left the trees at a run. The Mandan looked at the tracks, trotted to the edge of the trees, and could make out the tracks of the horse that cut across the flat and crossed the creek, mounting the ridge on the far side. He shook his head, knowing the running animal would be several miles away before he could fetch his own mount and give pursuit. One horse wasn't worth the effort. He looked at Big Devil and said, "Let's go to the camp!"

Beaulieux walked up beside the Mandan and Big Devil, handed a knife to the big Indian, "Since yours is still in that man's back, thought you might want this. He was skinning that elk with it." He looked at the pack horse, back at the carcass of the elk and suggested, "How 'bout we take that elk back to camp. We could use some fresh meat."

"Uhhnn," grunted Crow's Heart, nodding his head as he started back to the half-skinned cow elk.

19 / Taken

They had stripped Ezra of all his weapons, pistol, knives, and tomahawk, bound his hands behind him and pushed him at gunpoint into the camp, often prodding him with the muzzles of their rifles, so much so, that he stumbled twice and fell to his face. They forced him to rise without aid and prodded him onward. He wasn't surprised to see another man sitting in the camp, holding his rifle on the women as they worked at the fire, cooking a stew in the big pot and tending timpsila and camas bulbs roasting in the coals.

When they pushed Ezra before them into the camp, Dove jumped to her feet, started toward her man, but was stopped by the barked command from Beauchamp. "Git back here an' tend to your cookin'!" She scowled at the man but did as she was bidden.

"Wal, what do we have here? Didn't 'spect no

women!" declared the Métis, Marchand. "We gonna flip a coin for 'em?" he asked, grinning at the women, then glancing at Beauchamp.

"Only if you wanna get kilt!" growled Beauchamp, nodding toward the body of Ducette. "He thought he could handle one of 'em, and she gutted him!" he declared, motioning toward Otter, who refused to even look at the men, but busied herself at the fire.

"You don't say! Well, guess that's one less we hafta share with, ain't that what you wanted?" snarled Marchand. "I heard the two of you talkin' 'bout fewer shares. Guess he didn't figger on givin' up his share, did he?"

Beauchamp glared at Marchand, "Just keep your hands off them women. We'll take that negra and these women an' sell 'em for slaves. They'll fetch a good price that we'll all share, but they won't be worth nothin' if they're used up!"

Marchand looked to his two companions, men he had traveled with for several years, and grinned with a slight nod of his head that was understood by both men. He looked back at Beauchamp, "Whadaya want we should do with this 'un?" pointing at Ezra with his chin.

"Tie him up to that tree yonder, make it good an' tight. I don't wanna hafta put up with any of his shenanigans till after we teach him some manners," growled Beauchamp.

The three men pushed Ezra, making him stumble and fall again, then prodded him toward the tree at the edge of the camp. Marchand hit him from behind with the broad butt of his rifle, knocking him unconscious, forcing Moreau and Morgan to wrestle him around and tie him to the tree. He was regaining consciousness just as they finished binding him with the rawhide thongs, and as they started to walk away, Morgan kicked his leg, and jumped back when Ezra growled at him.

"Ha! What's he think he is, a bear or sumpin'?" laughed Morgan as he walked away.

Moreau dropped the four fish beside Dove, "Here's some fish your negra caught. You can fix 'em for our dinner!"

"He is my husband!" answered Dove through gritted teeth, glancing at the man who dropped the fish.

"Oh he is, is he? Well, he ain't gonna be nuthin' but a slave from now on. That's all his kind are good for anyway," retorted Morgan. He took a long look at Dove and Otter, lifted his eyes to Moreau and grinned, glancing back to the women with one raised eyebrow. He nodded toward Otter, then pointed at his chest, then toward Dove and nodded toward Moreau, indicating his choice of the women. Moreau shrugged and glanced at Beauchamp and Marchand, who were talking among themselves and paying little attention to the two. It was clear what they anticipated and planned, but their plan was yet to be formed, much less ready to implement.

The men had seated themselves near the fire as they watched the women at work, when the sound of approaching horses brought them to their feet, rifles in hand. Beauchamp motioned them to the trees as he spoke softly, "Prob'ly Crow's Heart and the others, but ready yourselves." He stood, back to the fire, rifle held across his chest as he craned around to see through the trees in the direction of the approaching horses. Crow's Heart was in the lead, followed by Beaulieux leading the loaded sorrel packhorse, then Big Devil, the Assiniboine. Beauchamp relaxed, sat his rifle down and watched as the three dismounted and tethered their horses with the others at the edge of the trees. He walked near and asked, "Well?"

"We kilt him like you said!" growled Beaulieux, "This 'un thought he'd do it with his knife, but I shot him in the head. He fell in the river and floated away, but not 'fore I put another bullet in his back!"

Crow's Heart added, "He killed an elk, we brought it," motioning to the deboned meat wrapped in the hide that Big Devil was taking down from the pack.

The women had watched as they entered the camp and recognized the sorrel. Dove looked at Otter and she nodded, whispering, "They don't have his black horse." But when Otter heard the report from the big

Frenchman, she drew a breath, and choked back a sob. She looked at Dove, then at Ezra, noticed Ezra shake his head slightly, but all their eyes were filled with fear and dread. Gabe could not be dead, he just couldn't, thought Otter. She was hoping the big man was mistaken and remembered to quietly say a prayer for her man.

When the horses had been stripped of their gear, the rest of the group walked to the fire, anticipating the meal the women were preparing. Crow's Heart stood looking at the women, then asked, "Who was the woman of that white man?"

Otter looked up and answered, "He is my husband."

"No more," growled the Indian, and threw the knife so it stuck in the log beside them. Otter looked to see and recognized the haft with the engraved guard and butt as that of Gabe's. She sucked a quick breath, put her hand to her mouth, and looked wide-eyed at the Mandan. He snarled, "Mebbe I take you for my woman!"

"Ain't nobody takin' either one of 'em! They're gonna be cookin' an' helpin' 'round camp is all they'll be doin'! We're gonna take care of 'em an' sell 'em with that slave yonder at the slave auction in St. Louis! They're worth more'n any load o' pelts we got, so if you want your share, you leave 'em alone!" demanded Beauchamp, looking at every man, eyes pinched and lip with a threatening snarl. "Got that?" he barked, looking from man to man for a nod of acknowledgment. "And know this, no matter who touches 'em, every other man needs to know that man is stealin' their share from 'em and better put a stop to it! Understand!" he shouted as he stood, swinging the muzzle of his rifle from one man to another.

There was no response or threat from anyone, so Beauchamp grunted, as he sat down. He looked at the women then snarled at his men again, "Sides, they might gut you like that one did Ducette."

The new arrivals to camp had not noticed the body of Ducette and looked where Beauchamp pointed with his chin to see the legs of the dead man protruding from behind the stack of gear, then looked at the woman who let a slow grin paint her face without looking at any of the men while she busied herself at the fire. She glanced at Ezra who was staring wide-eyed at her, then when she looked at him, he gave a slight nod of approval. Otter grinned and nodded, then turned back to the pot hanging above the fire.

Beauchamp looked around, "Beaulieux, after we eat, you take Big Devil, Morgan and Moreau, and go back to our other camp and bring up the rest of our gear and horses. We'll stay here till tomorrow to give the women time to smoke some o' that meat. Then we'll head out from here." He turned toward Crow's Heart, "You can scout out downstream, see if you find any other camps or villages. We'll be followin' this river back to the Missouri where we'll build us some boats and go downriver. We might even do that 'fore we hit the Missouri, depends . . ." he let the thought hang between them, offering a little hope of the soon coming end to their raiding and the beginning of their journey back to civilization and the garnering of the money for the goods and their share of the bounty.

There were grunts, mumbles and grins from the band, and all were a little more eager as they gathered close to the fire, ready to eat whatever the women had prepared. They were on the last leg of their journey and they began thinking about life away from the wilderness, complete with a sizable fortune to begin the next chapter of their lives. Each man had his own idea of what would be done with their pockets full of money and the thoughts varied from drunken brawls to wild parties to more reserved thoughts of having their own farm and home. But some were not thinking that far ahead, but as so many with no regard for others, their thoughts were more about the coming days and the nearby women.

20 / Retreat

The Métis, Marchand, had stepped into the number two position since the killing of Ducette. With the unquestioned loyalty of his two companions, he felt he had more of a claim to the leadership of the band of raiders, but he had yet to exercise what he felt was his opportunity. Choosing rather, to accede to the continued dominance of Beauchamp, at least until they were closer to the Missouri and their ultimate destination more of a true possibility, he felt it best to wait and watch, for there were others of concern. The big voyageur, Beaulieux, and the huge Assiniboine, Big Devil, who was appropriately named, and both of the men could easily be described as man mountains and both were loyal to Beauchamp. He had also heard Beauchamp talking with Crow's Heart, the Mandan scout, about a trading post near the Mandan village and it would be best to have Crow's Heart in alliance before he sought to usurp the authority of Beauchamp. He shrugged his shoulders as he thought of his options and decided to talk with his two companions before any action was taken.

Beauchamp led the straggly band, leading two packhorses. The twelve packhorses were divided among the rest of the bunch, with the Mandan alone on his scout. The three packhorses taken in their raid of the camp of the women and Ezra were led by Otter and Dove following. Ezra was sandwiched between the big Assiniboine and the voyageur, hands bound to the pommel and feet tied with a long rawhide under the belly of his horse. The women were in line between Marchand and Moreau, who took every opportunity to make snide remarks or lewd suggestions, both ending in his cackling laugh. Both women did their best to ignore his insinuations but when he rode up alongside Dove and reached out to touch her, she shouted and used the braided rawhide rein to smack him across his face, instantly raising a welt. He grabbed at his eyes, snarled and reached for her but was stopped by the shouts of both Marchand and Beauchamp. "I told you to keep your hands off those women! Next time I'll give her a knife an' let her hang your hide on her smoke racks! Got that?" shouted Beauchamp, shaking his fist and glaring at both him and Marchand. He looked directly at Marchand, "If you can't keep him in line, there'll be one less to share with! I ain't gonna put up with him!" he growled.

"I don't see what harm it'll do to let the men have a little fun, they are women and it ain't like they don't know what they're s'posed to do!" answered Marchand.

"Every time those women are touched, it costs us money! You think some white folks are gonna want a worn out and beat up squaw for a house slave?" he barked.

"Could always sell her to some tavern or house," suggested Marchand.

"That shows how much you know about the value of things. We could get two, three times the value for her as a house servant."

Marchand's eyes flared, then he turned back to Moreau, "Heed what he says! You're messing with our money!"

It was near the second day out from their camp when Crow's Heart sat waiting in the trail. When Beauchamp and Marchand came near he reported, "Crow village. Where two rivers meet. Big village, too big to fight."

"How many lodges?" asked Beauchamp.

Crow's Heart flashed both hands, all fingers so many times that Beauchamp lost count. He looked at Marchand, "That's a big village. I reckon he figgers over a hundred lodges." He sat for a moment, squinted his eyes as he looked at the scout, "Think they might wanna do some tradin'?"

"Mebbe. Mandan and Crow are enemies. Crow and Assiniboine are enemies."

"Well, I know you would like to kill some Crow and so would Big Devil, but you said there were too many. Maybe we," motioning to himself and Marchand, "could go into the village and do some tradin'." He looked at Marchand, "Whadaya think?"

"Well, that white man we killed had some trade goods, and we've got some things from the raid we could throw in on the deal, but you can't let them know we raided other Crow villages, so we'll need to keep the other horses and such outta sight," answered Marchand. "But, do you think the risk is worth it? I mean, what's to keep 'em from just slittin' our throats and take what we have?"

Beauchamp looked at Crow's Heart, "Is there a way around the camp, one that we could get by without a fight?"

"Mebbe, by Devil's Canyon trail, hard trail."

"We got too much to lose, so, let's give it a try," directed Beauchamp, frowning at the Indian.

"Need more daylight," suggested the scout, looking at the lowering sun. "Camp here, leave early."

"That village far enough away?" asked Marchand.

"Umm," grunted the Mandan, turning away, shaking his head.

"Go by night, safer," suggested Ezra, leaning forward on the pommel to relieve the tension in his arms caused by the constant tear of the rawhide bonds. His wrists were chafed raw, his ankles bloody, and his back bruised from the continual beatings with rifle stocks. The Frenchmen seemed to take a special delight in the beatings, having been deprived of the use of the women, they spent their energies driving Ezra to any task that required strength. Where many of the bales of furs were well over a hundred pounds, he was made to haul two at a time between the packs of the animals and the stacks. Forced to drag tree trunks to the fire and tasked with cutting and splitting the wood with the dull bladed axe, he was always under armed guard and taunted by his guards. At night he had his arms tied behind him and around a tree, almost dislocating his shoulder joints, and kicked by every passing guard. It wasn't until he slumped unconscious after being struck on the side of the head with a rifle butt by Moreau that Beauchamp did his best to put an end to the torture of the man. "He ain't no different than the women! If he's damaged goods, it'll cost us all!" He glared at the two most responsible for the mistreatment, Moreau and Morgan, "And if that happens, you'll lose your share, and that'll be several hundred dollars!" The mention of the money seemed to get their attention and after that, Ezra was treated a bit more humanely, but still like a slave who did most of the menial work around the camp.

Beauchamp glared at the black man, eyes squinted, then growled, "What do you know about travelin' at night?"

"We did it a lot. There'll be a full moon tonight, should be easy to find your way," answered Ezra.

"What do you care when we go?" asked Beauchamp.

Ezra chuckled, "If those Crow find us, you think they'll care who they kill? I don't want my scalp hangin' in some Crow lodge, and I don't want those women," nodding toward the sisters, "taken by the Crow."

"If they were taken by the Crow, might be better for 'em," suggested Beauchamp.

Ezra shook his head, "The Shoshone and Crow are enemies, they wouldn't be treated as good as a slave in a white man's house." He knew the Crow and the Shoshone were friendly, both Otter and Dove had told them before that there were times both tribes joined together for buffalo hunts and more, but he also believed Beauchamp knew little of the native bands.

Beauchamp slowly lifted his head to a slight nod, understanding the remark, but still distrustful of the man. He called out to Crow's Heart, "Hey scout! C'mere," and waited for the Mandan to return. Beauchamp looked at the man, "What about taking that trail by the moon?"

The scout lifted his eyes to the sky, thinking a moment, "Umm," nodding his head. He looked at the others, "Rest horses, leave when moon bright."

Beauchamp grinned, satisfied, then motioned the others to follow as he started for the thicker trees, mostly alder and willow, that offered sufficient cover for a cold camp, and some rest for the horses. There was ample graze nearer the riverbank and they would cross after dark. He stepped down and started stripping the gear from his horse, motioning the others to follow suit. Marchand cut the leg bonds on Ezra and once down, he tasked Ezra with stripping all the packhorses and taking them to water. He refused to remove the rawhide bonds on Ezra's wrists, and motioned for Morgan to guard the man.

"Make a cold camp, get some food ready but no fire," ordered Beauchamp as he approached the women. During the rides, they too had their wrists bound, but he removed the rawhides strips and allowed them to rub their wrists and go to work. They went to the parfleches and took out bundles of smoked meat, some corn dodgers, and took them to the big log in the middle of the clearing. Otter looked at Beauchamp, "I saw some berries that would be good. And there are some cattails and turnips. Should we go get them?"

Through squinted eyes and with his head cocked to the side, Beauchamp looked at the woman, trying to discern her motives. "You wouldn't be thinkin' 'bout runnin' away, would you?"

"No. But your men want to have good things to eat. We must gather them," answered Otter, stone faced.

Beauchamp looked at her, turned to Beaulieux, "You go with them. Don't take your eyes off 'em and let them get their berries and such."

The big man grinned, stood, picked up his rifle and motioned to the women to go before him. Otter and Dove picked up a small parfleche and started toward the river and the berries and more that would be used for the meals. Otter looked at Dove, lifted her head, and with that motion, said much. The women walked to the patch of strawberries Otter spotted earlier and knelt down to start gathering the red tidbits. Beaulieux stood close behind them, but soon bored of their scrounging in the greenery and looked for a more comfortable spot, finding one in the shade of a scrub cottonwood. He sat down, keeping his rifle pointed toward the women, but leaned back and relaxed. They were about ten or twelve yards away from the man, and turned their backs to him and Otter whispered, "I think Gabe is still alive. Wolf would have come back if he had not found him."

Dove's eyes widened as she looked at her sister, "If he's not hurt too bad, he will come for us!"

"Yes, but we must do what we can until he comes, and if he doesn't come," whispered Otter, grabbing at some berries. "I don't know how, but I will try to get a knife. You try too!"

21 / Recover

He felt like he had been crushed under a massive rockslide and at least one boulder had crushed his skull. Pain pushed through the darkness, something wet kept lapping at his head and face and he struggled to crack one eye. Blackness that moved before him caused his vision to swim and his head to hurt even more. He pinched his eye shut, struggled to open it again and saw dull red, a rough wetness clawed at his cheek and he tried to move, but his arms were beneath him, and he was under that pile of rocks, or was he? His right cheek seemed to be buried in something wet and rough. He tried unsuccessfully to lift his head but twisted a little and opened his other eye only to feel a few scratchy grains of sand try to force its way against his eyelid. He twisted a little, felt his shoulder move seemingly unhindered, and the wet roughness swiped at his face again. He forced his one eye wider and realized it wasn't darkness, but black fur! A bear? No, that must be Wolf!

He lifted one shoulder and drug an arm free, reaching for the black fur. The wolf jumped back, whined and licked his face again. Gabe was able to bury his fingers in the coat of his friend and use him to help pull himself up. Bright sunlight assaulted his squinted eyes and he hurt all over. His hand went to his head and felt the matted hair that had been the object of Wolf's licking and brought it before him to see some dried blood. He tried arching his back and felt a jabbing pain beside his right shoulder blade and remembered feeling the initial pain and standing and turning from his downed elk to see a grinning and mighty big Indian who held a bow at his side, nocking an arrow. Then he felt the impact to his head and remembered falling back into the water. He reached over his shoulder to try to feel the wound at his back but couldn't reach it. He tried bending his arm behind him and felt the dried blood at the edge of the wound. His twisting around brought pain from his hip and he looked down to see his buckskins gaping at his hip and saw more dried blood. But even with all the dried blood, there was fresh blood at every wound and blood on the sand beside him and in the middle of the small pool of blood lay the knife that had been in his back. His weakness told of losing considerable blood and he looked at the sun, barely above the eastern horizon, and he knew he had been here at least a day.

He looked around, saw he was on a sandbar, still wet up into the grasses, and guessed he had been caught in an excess runoff of snowmelt from the high country. He could tell by the high-water line on the banks of the creek that the usual flow was considerably less than what had carried him downstream. Gabe reached over and ran his fingers through the scruff of the wolf's neck, "Well, boy. Now what? I'm afoot," then he felt at his belt and was surprised to find his Bailes over/under pistol snagged in the tie and poking him in the belly, his possibles bag was over his shoulder and neck, but his powder horn was missing, "and have an empty and useless pistol." He felt at his waist for his hawk and knife, both missing, but he had the one from his back. Although it had a steel blade, it had probably been garnered in a trade or raid from some French-Canadian trader and was of lesser quality than his Flemish blade, but it would do until he could regain his blade, wherever it might be found. "And we're both afoot!"

He arched his back, felt the wound ooze some blood that trailed down his back. Then looked down at his hip, and felt his head, and knew he would have to do some tending to his wounds before he completely bled out. He glanced up at the blue sky, then down at Wolf, "At least you kept them," nodding to three circling turkey buzzards, "from picking my bones clean and I'm thankful for that, but let's see what we can find to tend these wounds." He struggled to his feet, looking around and grinned, Otter had taught him about several plants and he was pleased to see a tall skinny plant with a cluster of tiny yellow flowers and long skinny leaves that he recognized, goldenrod, or what had been called 'wound wort' since the times of the crusades. At the edge of the water were several willows and beyond that in the dry flats was an ample supply of sage.

He grimaced with the pain as he started to move, but he knew he had to survive. He also knew that if Ezra and the women could have come after him, they would have already found him. He looked at the surrounding terrain and recognized the tail end of the saddleback mountain that stood over their campsite and guessed himself to be no more than seven or eight miles from where they had camped. He bent down to pluck some goldenrod and the throbbing pain in his head drove him to his knees. He grabbed at the side of his skull, felt fresh blood and a groove cut through his scalp just above his ear. His flashback memory showed the big man that dropped the hammer on his rifle to send the bullet at him. Gabe had winced at the pain in his back just as the man shot or the bullet would have taken him in the forehead and he wouldn't be feeling pain now.

He breathed deep, forced himself to move, and plucked three plants of the goldenrod from the loose soil. He pushed himself up, and stood, a little wobbly at first, then walked to the willows. He twisted at a couple branches to break them free and began chewing on the inner bark. He would use the bark with the goldenrod and make a poultice for his wounds. He plopped down on a clump of grass that hung over the sandbar that had been his bed, stretched back for a big round rock with a flat side, and a smaller round river donie or stone that had been washed downstream and rounded smooth by the waters. He stripped the bark from the willow branches and began pounding them into a mush with the small stone, every blow jarring his head and sending sharp pains through his shoulder and hip. He then added the goldenrod, leaves, blooms, stems and all, and formulated a poultice.

He sat back, exhausted by the exertion, breathed deep and thought, about his wounds, his predicament, and his friends. He leaned forward, shook his head, reminding himself that worry was useless, and he must do everything he can to bind his wounds, get some strength back, and find out what happened. He lifted his eyes across the creek, saw a small bluff that rose about three hundred feet from the creek bed and thought that would be a good promontory, but would it be worth the effort, or should he conserve his strength for the walk back to camp? He busied himself with weaving a flat crisscross pad with the willow bark, something to hold the poultices to his wounds, and then stripped some lengths of fringe from his buckskins.

With a handful of poultice laid upon the first willow patch, he held it to the wound on his head, and one-handed draped a tied-together fringe strip over his head and over the pad. He secured it under his chin and once the pad was lightly secured in place, he used two more strips to make it more secure. He removed his buckskin top and after some twisting, turning and contortions, he managed to secure the patch to his back wound, then replaced his tunic. The efforts were repeated for his hip wound and once completed; Gabe lay back on the grass to regain some strength. He threw his arms to the side, eyes staring at the blue sky, but his fingers touched something strange and he turned to look. A patch of wild strawberries beckoned, and he sat up, reaching for the tasty tidbits and gathered them by the handfuls, tossing them into his mouth as he worked. He tossed some to Wolf who gladly bit down, but cocked his head to the side as he slowly chewed, giving Gabe a look like 'what are you feeding me?'

Although it seemed very little, the strawberries did offer a little strength, and he stood, looking around once again. He looked across the stream at the butte, back at the distant saddleback ridge, then upstream of the small creek. He chose to go upstream, hopefully find Ebony still tethered and waiting, although he wasn't too optimistic. The best he could imagine was that Ebony had pulled loose and not been taken by the big Indian and his equally sizeable friend. He glanced down to see if there were any more strawberries, saw none, and looked at Wolf, "Well, boy. Let's give it a try, shall we?"

The black wolf seemed to grin up at the man, wagged his tail and with tongue lolling took off with a bound. Every step seemed to jar his head and other wounds, but Gabe was driven by the need to know what happened with the others. He was hopeful of finding Ebony for the horse had learned to come at Gabe's whistle from the time the two were first together. Every time Gabe came to his stall or saw him in the pasture, he would whistle a two-cone call and the big black would lift his head and come running. He would nuzzle his rider and friend, nibble at him with his lips, searching for any kind of treat, whether a carrot, a handful of grain, or a clump of sugar. But he mostly reveled in the personal touch as Gabe would stroke his head and neck, always talking to him and becoming close friends.

Gabe had to stop often to sit and rest, to catch his breath, always searching for anything to eat and grabbed up some raspberries, a few bitter kinnikinnick berries, some rose hips, and some onions. With a couple short willow sticks in his belt, he chewed on the soft inner bark, knowing it held something that eased his pain. With each new try, he seemed to make a few more steps, and as he drew near where he downed the elk, he stopped, seated himself and started his whistle. But nothing moved, there was no answering whinny, no sound of anything but the water of the stream chuckling over the rocks and twisting its way to the larger river below.

He stood again and forced one foot in front of the other, moving wide of the thick brush and came to the meadow where he had hunted the elk. He leaned against a tree, whistled and waited, but there was nothing. He forced himself on, wanting to find where he was butchering the elk and hopefully find something else that would help him. Within several struggling moments, he spotted the break in the trees where the elk had watered and he staggered into the slight clearing, stumbled and fell to his knees. He sat back on his heels, looking around, and saw where the gut pile had been taken by the scavengers and carrion eaters, bits of hair was scattered beside the skull that had eyes, brains, and tongue taken. He sighed heavily and continued his survey of the scene. He remembered standing about where he was seated, had taken the knife in his back, then stood and was shot in the head. He absent-mindedly put his hand to the bandage above his ear and winced at the touch.

He looked around, trying to remember where the horses had been tethered and anything else he could think of when he thought about the Mongol bow. He twisted back to his left and looked at the rough barked cottonwood, then leaned forward a little and grinned. He pushed himself back to his feet and staggered over to the tree. There on the back side, still hanging from the broken branch were the bow and the quiver, untouched. He stretched up to reach the two and lifted them down from the hangar and held them close, glad that the assailants would never think of looking for a bow used by a white man. Now, with a weapon he could find meat and red meat was what he needed to restore his blood and strength.

22 / Trailing

When Gabe left home, his father had gifted him a pair of Flemish knives in a scabbard that held the pair. One was about thirteen inches with a drop point that he was using on the elk carcass when he was attacked and lost it, probably taken by his attackers. The other was about eight inches with a drop point and was still in the scabbard that hung at his back between the shoulder blades. He had found the knife that the Indian had thrown into his back and had slipped that into the scabbard with the smaller Flemish knife. After retrieving his Mongol bow and quiver of arrows, he knew he could take some much-needed meat. But now he was tired and needed a bit of rest and needed to do a little planning as well.

He stepped away from the stream and into the thicker trees, found a small clearing and started to stretch out on the grass, but his thoughts lingered on the missing stallion, Ebony. He stepped to the edge of the trees and let loose his usual two-toned whistle, first one direction then the other, hoping to hear the customary answering whinny from his horse and to see him come running. But there was nothing, no whinny, no thundering hooves, nothing that spoke of the presence of the big black. Gabe returned to the small clearing, stretched out in the shade of a tall ponderosa, and fluffed up a bed with the dry needles for Wolf and himself, put his hands behind his head and closed his eyes, hoping for some elusive rest. Wolf pushed up against the warmth of the man, content with his friend.

It had been about two hours, but it seemed like a few short moments, when Wolf let a low rumble come from deep within, stirring Gabe awake. But the man did not move anything but his eyes, searching the trees nearby for movement or sound. He slowly sat up, reaching for his bow and quiver, then went to his knees when he saw movement at the break in the trees where the trail led many to water. A young buck, wary and alone, tiptoed to the water, big ears moving first forward then back, eyes searching. Then he slowly dropped his nose to the water for a quick drink, lifted again and looked around. When his head was down, Gabe moved just a little to the left for a better clearing and opening to shoot.

The buck paused, one foot lifted, then slowly

lowered his head for another drink. When his head was down, Gabe struggled to bring the bow to a full draw but had to release sooner than he wanted because of his waning strength. The arrow whispered toward its mark and buried itself into the neck of the buck just as he started to step back from the water. Gabe had aimed at the lower chest, but the arrow still struck true and the buck staggered, tried to bleat, and fell to the side, kicking.

Gabe waited a moment until the animal stopped moving, then he rose and walked closer. He poked the buck in the side with his toe, then knelt down, put his hand on the warm neck and softly said, "Thank you for giving your life so I could live. If you hadn't come along, I might not have lasted much longer." He lay his bow on the neck of the buck and began the arduous task of dressing the animal out. He cut the liver free, sliced off a strip and dipped it in the bile, and ate it raw. The iron-rich meat was what he needed, cooked or not; he couldn't wait. He ate another strip and sat back to rest a few moments before finishing the butchering. He took a deep breath, stood to his feet and walked to the water, went to hands and knees for a deep drink, and satiated his thirst.

He stood, looked around, whistled again, and again, heard nothing and returned to the carcass. He threw some scraps to Wolf and watched as he quickly devoured the fresh meat. He looked overhead and saw a chicken hawk circling, a couple buzzards drifting on the wind, and heard the scream of an eagle. All were waiting their turn at the kill.

Gabe took the backstraps, the loins, choice cuts from the hind quarters and chose to leave the rest for the many scavengers, knowing that by this time tomorrow, there would be little evidence of a kill. He bundled the meat into a patch of hide and went back to the little clearing. His possibles bag was finally dry, but the tinder inside was not. He took his flint and steel out, laid it aside and went looking for some tinder. A dead snag of a cottonwood had a hole near the ground and a quick inspection revealed some fine nesting material that would make good tinder. He took it and began gathering up small sticks and soon had a fire going, small, but useful. With thin strips of back strap dangling from green willow withes, the small flames licked at the sizzling meat and Gabe's meal was a little rare, but quite tasty to a very hungry man.

Gabe was leaning back against the big tree, waiting for his second round of strip steaks to cook a little more, when Wolf suddenly jumped to his feet, head down, eyes squinting, but making no sound, no growling, no rumbling, and Gabe looked where the wolf was looking but saw nothing. He picked up the bow and nocked an arrow as he came to his knees, but Wolf took off at a run, twisting through the trees like he was in pursuit of a fleeing jackrabbit, and quickly disappeared beyond the timber. But within moments, Gabe saw the wolf running and jumping, tongue lolling and drool dripping as he bounced through the trees returning to his friend. Behind him came a shadowy figure that was soon recognized as Ebony!

Gabe shouted, "Ebony! Come here boy!" and dropped his bow to the side and ran to the edge of the trees to greet his friend. The big black stretched out his head, reins trailing and high stepping around them, lips flapping as if he was talking and greeting his friend, and Gabe threw his arms around the stallion's neck and hugged him tight, thankful and excited. He rubbed the big horse's neck, talking to him and running his fingers through his briar tangled hair. He stepped back, saw dried lather under the breast collar and girth, and led the horse into the clearing and began stripping off the saddle. He was relieved to see the Ferguson rifle secure in the scabbard and the saddle pistols in their holsters at the pommel. He dropped the saddle to the ground, and snatched up some grasses to rub the big, beautiful beast down. Both man and horse enjoyed this time of intimacy and friendship, and the horse especially appreciated being rid of the gear. After the rubdown, Ebony rolled in the grass, stood, shook all over and stepped closer to the man and nibbled at his arm with those big lips.

Gabe put his forehead on the forehead of his horse and held him close, speaking softly to his friend.

He now knew he would be all right. He had his weapons, could regain his strength and had his horse. But now the question to be answered was 'What happened to Ezra and the women?' He had seen the tracks of those that attacked him and knew they turned back to where the camp lay and probably had attacked them as well, but he did not know how many were in the bunch and what had happened to his friends. But this time the element of surprise would be on his side, for they surely thought him dead and would not be expecting any retaliation from him.

He lifted his eyes to the sky, guessed there to be about three hours of daylight left, and also knew there would be a full moon tonight. Although weak, he had to put that aside and find his friends. He finished his meal, checked his weapons and used the spare powder horn to reload all the pistols and his rifle, then saddled up and stepped aboard. He reached down and patted the black on the neck, looked down at Wolf, and said, "Fellas, we've got to find Ezra and the women, let's go!" Wolf started off at a long lope, bounding over the trail that led back to the camp where the four of them were last together. Ebony stretched out and followed, his gait an easy canter, but covered the ground quickly. Once across the wide meadow, Gabe reined up and turned into the trees. A small stream paralleled the mountain and cut through the timber directly into the clearing used as a camp, but they would not charge into the camp unknowing. When within about a hundred and fifty yards of the campsite, Gabe reined up and stepped down. He ground tied Ebony, slipped one of the double-barreled saddle pistols into his belt alongside the over/under Bailes, hung the quiver of arrows at his side, nocked one in the bow and started forward.

Gabe could move as silently as any Indian, when he worked his way through the trees, picking every step carefully, never turning a stone or crushing a leaf or needle, never brushing a branch or trunk. He moved like a lithe panther, and the sunlight sent shafts of brilliance between the trees and the golden rays danced before the shadow that moved from tree to tree. When the clearing came into view, it was easy to see it had been abandoned. Nothing moved, no smoke came from the fire circle, a whiskey jack bounced among tidbits left behind. Gabe relaxed and walked forward, looking at the tracks and other sign. It was easy for him to distinguish the different tracks, those of the women, Ezra, and the others. The strange horses and footprints of other men told the story in the dust, his friends had been taken captive, but at least they were alive.

Then Gabe heard the sound of a badger snarling at some other creature and he walked closer. The striped creature of the woods was standing his ground against a cowardly coyote as they fought over the remains of a man. The body had already been picked over by buzzards, lynx, ravens, and other carrion eaters, but the badger and coyote were fighting over the remains. Gabe turned away, but something caught his eye and he walked closer to the body. One foot still had a moccasin, but it was of the type and beading Otter had described as Crow. He pushed at it with his toe, the badger snarling and not moving, then he saw what he was certain was the remains of a scalp at the belt, or what remained of the belt, of the man. He was not a Crow, but a white man, and based on what had happened when he was attacked and now the evidence at the camp, Gabe knew these were renegades, probably traders and trappers that had chosen what they saw as the easy way to make their fortune. Leaving the creatures to their stand-off, satisfied the body was of an unknown white man, undoubtedly one of the attackers that had been killed by one of his friends. Little did he know that it was his woman, Pale Otter, who had done the deed.

As he read the story in the dirt, he saw where the three had come from the direction of his kill and attack and later left. The others had spent the night and Ezra had been tied to a tree, the women tied nearby. As he walked to the edge of the clearing, he saw where some had returned, leading a string of packhorses, and the entire group had left, following the river.

He went back into the trees and brought the horse and wolf to the campsite. He chose to cook up some more meat, wanting to travel through the night without having to stop, and get a little rest for him and the horse before starting the pursuit. He had a feeling this was going to be a long hunt and a challenging one at best. Near as he could figure with the myriad of tracks, there were at least seven or eight men, over a dozen horses, many of them pack animals, and all of them experienced woodsmen. The task before him was daunting, but he had little choice. They had his wife and his friends, and he vowed they would regret ever making that mistake that would probably cost them their lives.

23 / Trek

The women portioned out the berries to all the men but reserved the onions, camas bulbs, and timpsila for later when they would be a welcome addition to a hot meal. As Otter was packing the new vegetables into the parfleche, she remembered that among the trade goods Gabe and Ezra had packed along were a number of knives that were always a welcome trade item among all the tribes. With a glance over her shoulder at the men, some snoozing, others munching on their latest treat of a handful of berries, she casually made her way to the packs with the trade goods.

She started rummaging through the pack then heard a voice from behind her, "What'chu lookin' for?" It was Morgan, leaning against a nearby tree, watching. He stepped forward, "Lookin' for these?" he asked, holding three trade knives out toward her.

"No, no, I . . . uh . . . I need some cord to tie the timpsila together. They dry better that way, the camas too," she declared, turning her back to him and searching for some cord. She found a roll and dug it out, held it up for him to see then pushed by him to return to the parfleche with the vegetables. She made busy tying the bundles, glancing at Dove and giving a slight shake of her head that was understood by her sister.

Dusk was dropping the curtain of darkness when Beauchamp called out, "All right, let's load 'em up. We've got to get outta here 'fore the Crow come snoopin' an' find us!"

The men mumbled and grumbled but rose to their feet and started to the horses. Moreau untied Ezra's hands from behind the tree, held the rifle on him while Morgan wrapped the rawhide thongs around his wrists, then prodded him up to start loading the bales of pelts onto the packhorses. Once everything was loaded, Beauchamp nodded to Crow's Heart and watched the Mandan scout gig his mount into the river's edge to cross over.

It was a lazy current and shallow water, although still muddy from the runoff, and the moonlight bounced off the ripples, dimpling the shadows with the reflected light. The six men each led two packhorses, Otter led the two mustangs, Dove the sorrel, and Ezra struggled with his bound wrists and feet tied together under the belly of his horse. The cavalcade muddied the water even more, but the muddy runoff would show no difference by the time the waters reached the Crow encampment.

They followed the dry creek bed in the bottom of a deep ravine that cut its way through the dry adobe soil of the foothills. The lazy moon hung in the eastern sky giving light to the travelers. Even in the ravine bottom, the moon bent its light to show the way. The twisting gully turned around a low ridge, crossed a wide flat, then took them into a cut between two rocky hills that stood as sentinels at each end of a razor back ridge. Once around the point of the ridge, the dry creek bed petered out but the way was open to a well-used ancient trail that took them to a narrow grassy valley that carried a live stream of mountain run-off to the river below.

They had come a little less than ten miles when they stopped at the stream that Crow's Heart referred to as 'Crooked Creek', and Beauchamp called for a short break. "Water the horses, loosen 'em up a little, and step out a bit. The scout says the next part is a bit rougher, so we want the horses rested a mite."

Moreau loosened Ezra's bonds so he could get down, not because of any concern for him but for the horse. Ezra sat down on a nearby stone, stretched his legs and rubbed his ankles, and started to sit back when he heard the lonesome call of a wolf, high up on the hill. He glanced over to Otter who was looking into the shadows, but both knew it was not the call of her black Wolf. Yet that call was soon answered by another that came from farther down their backtrail, high on the ridge they crossed and this sounded more familiar. They didn't know for sure, but they were hopeful as they looked at one another, letting slight grins split their faces.

They crossed Crooked Creek into the dry land of burnt umber, the dark orange soil was clay-like and held no vegetation. A slight rise dropped into a veritable wasteland that stretched a mile toward dry foothills. The trail rode the shadows of a rising hill where a few scraggly piñon clung with tenuous footholds to the steeper slopes scarred by some ancient runoff that carried loose soil to mound together at the base. A cairn stood at the juncture of two ancient trails, that marked a gulley that twisted out of sight as it climbed into the taller foothills. Nearby, freckles of green showed on the hillside where more piñon marched up the narrow ravines.

Beauchamp followed close behind Crow's Heart, with Marchand next in line. Both men led two packhorses, as did the others. Ezra rode alone, hands still tethered to the pommel of his saddle and every rocking sway of the animal rubbed the stiff leather of the saddle against his bound legs, making the raw skin protest with each step. With wrists and ankles chafed and raw, the insides of his legs even more tender, he struggled to keep from crying out in pain, but he was determined to show no fear or agony nor give his captors any satisfaction in their tormenting of him. He had to steel himself against their torture and watch for any opportunity to escape. He was more concerned for Dove and Otter, although they had not been severely mistreated, he didn't believe that Beauchamp could long keep the others from the women. Ezra shook his head at the thought and struggled with his bonds, but each move seemed to tighten the rawhide thongs rather than loosen them. He arched his back to stretch the bruised muscles and loosened his shoulders as he moved back and forth. He lifted his eyes to the big moon, now stretching the shadows of the piñon on the slopes and remembered the many nights he and Gabe had traveled by the light of the lonesome midnight lantern. The pleasant thought brought a grin and he twisted in his seat to look to the back trail, wondering if his friend was following.

***

Gabe figured he was about a day, maybe more, behind the band of raiders. He put Ebony into a ground eating canter, letting him stretch his long legs on the easy trail that paralleled the Shoshone river, the big moon offering all the light they needed to make good time. There had been no effort on the part of the raiders to obscure their trail, even if it were possible to cover the tracks of what Gabe thought were at least twenty-four horses. By the sign, he knew they were not traveling fast, but neither did they make too many stops. At each camp, he scoured the tracks for any evidence of his friends or any mistreatment of them. The most he found were bloodied rawhide strips that had probably been used to bind the prisoners. There were no bits of ripped or torn buckskins that would tell of an assault on the women, nor any items left behind.

Until he came to the second camp beside the Shoshone, he had found nothing to give extra hope, nor anything that would cause alarm. It was there he found tracks of the women away from the camp near a picked over patch of strawberries. Two strings of fringe were tied together, one with a white tuft of rabbit fur and white and blue beads, the other with yellow and white beads. Otter had fringe with the blue and white and Dove had the other two colors. Gabe grinned as he recognized the sign that Otter was saying the sisters were together and leaving sign for him to follow. That meant they believed he was coming for them. He grinned as he stuffed the fringe in his pocket, walked back to where Wolf and Ebony waited, Ebony munching on the tall grass at the edge of the trees and Wolf chewing on a scrap of meat.

They had been traveling fast and Gabe knew Ebony needed some rest to stay fresh, but he was too antsy to just sit and wait. He swung aboard the big black, pointed him to the river and started across. Wolf splashed into the water behind them and in short order they climbed the far bank, but the brief crossing gave Gabe pause as he felt a little light headed. He reined up, walked Ebony to the edge of some willows and stepped down. He rolled out his blankets, loosened the girth on the saddle, picketed the horse close by and with rifle at his side, stretched out to get some rest. He knew he and Ebony as well as Wolf, needed to stay fresh. If they came on the raiders and couldn't give chase, it would all be for naught and the women and Ezra would be further threatened. With his hands behind his head, he stared at the few remaining stars and voiced a simple prayer for God's strength and guidance for both him and his friends. As he drifted off to sleep, he realized he was gritting his teeth in anger at the idea of Otter in the hands of one of the raiders, and he asked himself if it was right for him to pray that God would let him take vengeance upon the captors?

It was late morning when Gabe awoke. Nothing stirred, Ebony stood three-legged facing into the willows, eyes closed and head hanging slightly. Wolf's eyes opened when Gabe stirred, and the black wolf watched as Gabe scanned his surroundings. Satisfied, Gabe slowly rose from his blankets, picked up the Ferguson, and went to the saddle bags for some of the cooked strip steaks left from the previous night's meal. After leading Ebony to the water for a long drink, he tightened the cinch, slipped the Ferguson in the scabbard, and swung aboard. He was not aware of the big Crow village that was nestled in the valley at the mouth of the Shoshone, but that was about five miles downstream and he was only concerned about the trail of the raiders.

The dry creek bed was bottomed with powdery silt that puffed with each footfall of the big stallion. Dry land stretched out on both sides, little or no vegetation save cacti of assorted types. Spiny cholla clawed at the suffocating heat, stretching like aerated skeletons for any moisture in the desert wind. Prickly pear clustered together, the red apple buds having shed the yellow petals of early blossoms, and the broad barbed blades starting to shrivel in the heat. The hot sun showed no mercy on the black horse and his rider, moving at a long-stride quick step, a dust cloud chasing. Gabe's head hung as his cottony mouth held his dry tongue captive. Wolf kept pace, his tongue lolling and head hanging, and Gabe knew the two animals with their coats of black were feeling every bit of the heat and more.

When they dropped from the ridge, the tall razor back gave a brief respite with the long shadow that covered the trail. Gabe reined up and stepped down, took a drink from his water bag and poured some into his hand for Wolf, then more into his hat for Ebony. He splashed the remainder on his face and neck, replaced the stopper in the bladder bag and hung it from the pommel. He breathed deep, then put a foot in the stirrup, grabbed the pommel, and as he started to swing aboard, he heard and felt the whisper of an arrow barely missing his shoulder as it flew past. The screams of war cries sounded, and a quick glance told Gabe there was a war party after him. Ebony needed no encouragement and lunged forward, almost unseating Gabe, but he held on, lay low on the stallion's neck and they went at an all-out run for the valley bottom that carried Crooked Creek.

24 / Fight

The big stallion stretched out and began to put a little distance between them and the Crow war party. Gabe lay low along the black's neck, the long mane whipping at his face, but he lifted enough to see there was little cover offered. He twisted around to look at his pursuers and saw a small band, his quick glance telling him they numbered maybe five or six. He had no idea how fresh the horses of the warriors were, but he knew an extended chase in this heat could hurt Ebony and his chances of catching the raiders. The trail dipped into a small gulley, climbed the other side and Gabe slid Ebony to a stop and pulled the stallion's head around as he grabbed one of the saddle pistols, cocking both hammers and dug his heels into the ribs of the black to charge directly at the Crow war party.

The five warriors had just dropped into the gully

when Gabe and Ebony crested the high side and charged down among them. Trusting Ebony to find his own way, offering a little guidance with his knee pressure, Gabe snatched the second pistol from the holster and fired at the first warrior, saw red blossom on his chest then turned toward the second and dropped the hammer on the second barrel. The second warrior rolled to the side when the big lead ball punched a hole in the side of his head, but Gabe was already focused on the next warrior. The remaining three had swung their horses around in the bottom of the draw, but Gabe had already brought his second pistol to bear and fired once, twice, as the group of three were clustered together. As Ebony climbed the trail out of the gully in three long fast strides, Gabe jammed both empty pistols into their holsters and drew the over/under Bailes pistol from his belt as he turned Ebony back for another charge. A quick glance showed one man slumped on the neck of his horse, another showing red at his shoulder, the third lifting a lance to charge their attacker. Gabe reined up Ebony and waited just an instant for the Crow to draw near then fired his first barrel at the charging man.

The warrior dropped to the side of his mount just as Gabe fired and with a handful of mane and his heel hooked behind the edge of his makeshift saddle, the screaming warrior rode past. Gabe quickly spun the barrels on the pistol, cocked the second hammer and kicked Ebony towards the warrior who was now upright and readying to charge. Gabe bent low, but brought the Bailes in line and fired, surprising the warrior with the lead ball splitting his hair-bone breastplate, and penetrating his chest, knocking him backwards off the charging horse.

Gabe spun around, looking for the others, jammed the pistol in his belt and slipped the Ferguson from the scabbard. He walked Ebony to the edge of the gully, looked down to see a lone warrior, still mounted, holding his arm with blood running between his fingers. The man glared at Gabe, waiting for him to shoot, but Gabe gigged the big stallion down into the draw and up the other side, never taking his eyes off the man who continued to stare. Gabe stopped Ebony, turned to face the warrior, nodded and slipped his rifle into the scabbard, then turned and trotted off. The warrior's eyes flared as Wolf came from the side and followed close behind.

They rode to the narrow valley of Crooked Creek, reined up beside the stream and with a long look at his back trail, stepped down to refill his water bag and let Ebony take a long drink. Once the stallion's thirst was slaked, and Wolf had bellied down on the cool sandy bank, he trusted them to watch for danger while he put his face in the water, splashed the back of his neck, and sat back on his heels to look around. He was still on the trail of the raiders, they had crossed the creek at this same spot, but he was concerned about the war party. If they were near a village, he knew it was probable the lone survivor could return to the village and his report might prompt another war party to come after him, and it would be an easy undertaking since the trail he was following could be found by a blind man in a snow storm. Although the usual priority would be to recover the bodies of the dead, if the village was large enough, they could also mount enough warriors to give pursuit and seek vengeance. He shook his head at the thought of his concern about taking vengeance himself, but now he might be on the receiving end and that wasn't too reassuring.

With another scan of his back trail, he took the time to reload all his weapons, always vigilant for any pursuit. Wolf had trotted off, probably to find himself a jackrabbit for his dinner. The sun was cradled in the crests of the western mountains, lances of gold and orange shot into the fading blue sky, and Gabe started on the trail into the dry lands. The burnt umber soil beckoned, and the trail crossed the wide flat, and pointed up a winding draw, just past the stacked rock cairn that marked the way. He leaned down to look at the trail a little closer, seeing the dried clumps of soil that had been turned by the many passing horses, but a pile of horse apples at the side of the trail, shaded slightly by the sage beside the trail, were still dark and damp on the bottom, meaning it had been no more than twelve daylight hours since those horses passed.

He sat upright in the saddle, stood in his stirrups to look further up the trail, but saw nothing of importance and dropped into the seat and spoke to Ebony, "Well boy, we're gainin' on 'em. Now if we can stay ahead of any o' them Crow that want to come after us, and not warn the raiders, well, hopefully we can do some good." He shook his head at his present predicament and knew if Ezra were here he could chide him considerably for always getting them into trouble, but as he saw it, Ezra was in the toughest fix.

***

The trail made a steady climb up the long-slanted face of the low shoulder that came from the mountains to their west. Sagebrush, greasewood, rabbit brush, and thistles all competed for what little water was held in the deep adobe and sandstone soil. A love sick coyote barked from the darkness, ending his cry with the yip-yip-yip so common to his kind. A few moments later an answer came from further up the trail and the furry tailed coward of the flats scampered over the rocks in pursuit of his nighttime rendezvous. The horses plodded along, feeling the warmth from the

soil that caught the days sweltering heat and held it
into the darkness. The cool of the night was made
temperate by the low breeze that worked its way
up from the depths of the nearby canyon. The usual
quiet of the night was accompanied by the roaring
and crashing of the white water in the deep gorge as
it echoed back and forth between the limestone walls.

The trail dipped into a steep sided ravine,
obviously cut by flash floods rushing to meet the
white water below, moonlight shadows dimpled the
banks, and the gravelly bottom of the ravine caused
several horses to stumble but none fell. Taut lead
lines gave the animals additional footing and the
cavalcade rose from the bottom to follow the narrow
hanging trail beside the canyon walls. Crow's Heart
had waited beside the trail for Beauchamp, "Bad Pass
Trail, very narrow, loose rocks, go slow," he directed,
and without waiting resumed the lead.

Beauchamp turned to pass the word to Marchand,
who passed it on behind him. Each man gave his
follower the caution, and the entire group spaced
out and moved slowly, giving plenty of lead line to
any trailing animals. Beaulieux followed Marchand,
leading two heavily loaded pack animals. He was
a man used to forcing his will on others or bulling
his way through fights or arguments and was out of
sorts taking orders from others. When one of the
horses balked a little, the big man, always uneasy in

the darkness and riled by the demands of Beauchamp and others, angrily jerked on the lead line. Beaulieux had done exactly what he had been warned not to do by tying the lead rope of the packhorses to his pommel, leaving his hands free for whatever activity he felt was more important. But when the pack animal balked, he reached down and jerked with all his weight, thinking to exert his will on what he considered to be a dumb animal. But the packhorse had balked at a rattlesnake, and although it wasn't coiled and rattling, it startled the horse.

When the big man jerked on the rope, the horse stepped back, leaning his full weight on the line and pinning the big man's leg to the saddle. But Beaulieux, ox that he was, lifted the line and swung his leg over the rump of his horse to step to the ground. When he did, the loose rock slipped from under his feet and he fell face down and began sliding to the edge of the canyon. He scrambled, shouted, and kicked as he grabbed at a piece of greasewood, uprooting it, then caught the hoof of the pack animal who kicked at him, striking him in the face and sending him closer to the edge. He finally found a grip on a rough edge of rock that stopped his descent, but the startled horses were kicking and fighting their way back to the trail and loosened several rocks that tumbled into Beaulieux's face and eyes. His grip slipped on the rocks and he slid over the edge, his scream muffled by the roar of the rapids in the bottom of the canyon. Sound always carries further in the night air and the scream of the terrified man bounced between the canyon walls, sounding as if there were dozens of men falling to their death. A thud, then another scream followed by a more distant impact, then all that was heard were the sounds of the crashing water echoing in the gorge.

Ezra had been behind Beaulieux and his packhorses but was smart enough to keep a good distance between them. When the horses spooked, Ezra's bay stepped back, and he held him still as they watched the drama of the big man play out before him. Had he been unhindered, Ezra would probably have been able to help the man, but bound as he was, there was nothing he could do but watch. Although Beaulieux had not been as sadistic as the others, he had not been a help and his advances toward Otter and Dove had been threatening and unwelcome. Although it was never a good thing to see a man die, Ezra felt no remorse for the man.

Marchand had hurriedly dismounted and tossed the lead lines to his horses to Beauchamp as he turned to grab the reins and leads of the horses of Beaulieux. He saw the big man fall and scramble as he slid to the edge, but before Marchand could get to him, even if he tried, the man was gone. Marchand was more concerned about the packhorses and the bales of furs they carried, for that was part of their bounty and would now have one less to share with, and he grinned in the darkness as he thought about the big man and his fall into the gorge, all the while thinking how his share was growing.

The rest of the group showed all the necessary caution, taking the hazardous trail slowly and carefully, often talking to the horses to give reassurance both to the horses and themselves. With no further incidents, and the trail moving away from the edge of the gorge, the group made a few more miles before Crow's Heart pointed them into a coulee that held a narrow stream and some alders, willows and a smattering of cottonwood. Beauchamp agreed it would make a good camp and they could even have a fire. As Otter and Dove stepped down, Otter froze in place when she heard the lonesome cry of a wolf, far up on the slope of the long timber covered ridge, so distant she almost didn't hear it, but the familiar cry brought a smile to her face and she nodded to her sister who had also heard the cry of the wolf. The sun was breaking over the eastern horizon, splashing color across the dull blue and grey, as the women gathered some firewood to start the morning meal. Everyone was relieved and tired, but Ezra was concerned after overhearing a conversation between Marchand and his two partners about him taking over soon.

25 / Close

This was strange country to Gabe, so dry that every footfall added another layer of dust to his shoulders and gear and each breath was choked into a cough. With nothing but sage, greasewood and rabbit brush casting shadows twice their height, the moonlight distorted the lay of the land. He looked between the ears of the big stallion, his head bobbing with each step, searching for visible sign of the trail that was shouldered nearer the black scar that told of a river canyon. Unfamiliar with the country, he recognized the roar of the river coming from a deep gorge and did his best to stay shy of it, but Ebony picked his steps on the ancient trail, following the tracks of the raiders and their captives.

The big moon grinned at the lone traveler and shed its light on the trail, often stretching shadows into distorted images made alive by a tired mind and weary, still weakened, body. Ebony dropped over the bank of the steep-sided ravine, catching Gabe off guard, but he leaned back, bending over the high cantle of the dragoon saddle. Rocks and gravel rattled across the bottom and when Ebony started up the opposite and steep bank, Gabe leaned forward over the pommel, catching a handful of mane. Once atop, Ebony paused, and both man and horse heard the sounds of roaring water cascading over rocks and rapids far below in the black void of the canyon. The hanging trail gave little room for maneuvering as the sure-footed Andalusian stallion stepped lightly, seldom glancing in the direction of the roaring river. As they started up the incline that pointed the trail away from the canyon, the loose gravel slipped beneath the big black and he fell to his knees, almost pitching Gabe over his head, but Ebony did not move until Gabe regained his seat and balance. When Gabe leaned far back on the high tall cantle, Ebony heaved himself to his feet and clamored up the incline. Both horse and man breathed deeply once on the wider trail away from the edge and Gabe leaned down to pat Ebony's neck, "Good boy, Ebony, good boy."

Wolf had been sitting at the side of the trail, appearing like another shadow in the blue light of the moon, but when his friends stopped, he stepped forward as Ebony dropped his head to the wolf and greeted his friend. "Well, glad to see you could join us, Wolf. I thought you had gone huntin' your supper, but I don't see anything." With a wave of his hand, Gabe motioned Wolf ahead and the trio resumed their journey.

The trail moved away from the gorge and the roar of the rapids in the canyon dimmed. On the flats, the moonlight danced between the clumps of sage and stretched the shadows of the greasewood. A long eared jackrabbit startled both horse and rider when it sprang from under the nearby clump and the shadowy form of Wolf gave chase. A coyote tried to cut in on the dance and was tumbled end over end by Wolf who didn't miss a step as he twisted around the sage and rabbit brush. Gabe was reminded of the tune played by the fiddlers and concertina aboard the flatboat on the Ohio River as the pilgrims square danced to the tune called by the yodeling master. The long eared jackrabbit disappeared in a cloud of dust when Wolf caught his supper and held on through the tumble. As they drew near, Gabe chuckled at the wolf as he ripped and tore at the long legs of the snowshoe jackrabbit.

The trail dipped into a coulee that held a trickle of a stream that chuckled over the gravelly bottom and Gabe pointed Ebony upstream, staying in the water and pushing through the willows. He was still concerned about the Crow war party and if they would pursue him. He knew any good tracker could still follow their trail in the stream because the hooves of the horse dug deep and once the mud was washed downstream, the disturbed gravel would be a giveaway. But if they did come, he hoped they would be more focused on the tracks of the twenty or more horses of the raiders and might overlook where he left the trail. He was searching for a place to bed down, for it had been a long day and night's travel and both man and horse could use some rest. He felt the bandage at his head, found it secure and dry, but the one at his hip was damp with blood. He would have to replace the poultices and bandages, but he felt the wounds were healing well. Otter had told him that the clear mountain air was good for wounds and promoted quick healing and he was beginning to realize the truth of her words.

He held to the stream for almost a mile, then a wide patch of rock offered a way out and he stayed on the solid rock mound that rose to a higher knob of a hill. Once on the hilltop, he saw the wide shoulder of the long timber covered ridge that rose high above the flats and the river gorge. He stood in his stirrups, looking at the flatland and the ribbon of the trail, then satisfied, pointed Ebony to cross another dry creek bed and stopped at a line of scrub piñon. He stepped down and stretched, then stripped the gear from the black, and rolled out his blankets. He watched as the stallion rolled in the dry grass and dirt, stood and shook, then walked to the edge of the trees. Buffalo grass grew in clumps on the lee side of the trees and Ebony was soon taking his fill.

From his vantage point above the flats and the valley beyond, even in the moonlight, Gabe got a good idea of the trail ahead and the terrain that waited. He hoped to see the winking light of a campfire that would tell of the presence of the raiders, but there was nothing. Wolf had trotted off and moments later, Gabe heard the mournful cry that can only come from a lonesome wolf and knew Wolf was calling to Otter. Gabe dug some strips of leftover meat from his saddle bags and sat on his blankets, looked at the vast land before him, and began to talk with his God.

***

"That Beaulieux wasn't very considerate when he decided to take a bath in that canyon back yonder," said Marchand, poking at the cookfire with a stick, wanting to use it to light his clay pipe.

"What'chu mean?" asked Beauchamp, scowling.

"Wasn't he the one that knew how to build the boats?"

"Uh, yeah, but 'fore we knew 'bout that we were gonna build rafts, so, reckon we can still do that," grumbled Beauchamp.

Marchand lit his pipe, took a deep draw as he stared into the flames, then looking at Beauchamp, "Ever built bullboats?"

"Yeah, when we was with the Northwest comp'ny and went on that foray on the Peace River, we brought back some stuff in a bunch o' bullboats."

"The Mandan use 'em all the time. I was talkin' to Crow's Heart an' he said that when this river gets outta the canyon, that there's good buffalo country. For every buff we take, we can make a bull boat, an' they ain't that hard to build. Prob'ly only take a couple days to build enough of 'em, an' when we tie 'em together, they'll be easier to take downriver."

Jacques Beauchamp stared at the fire, brow furrowing, then glanced at Marchand, "You might have an idea there. I know it takes one buffler hide to make a bullboat, but I seem to remember some voyageur sayin' you could use two and make it more like a batteaux, but you hafta waterproof the seam. Might be too much trouble cuz I shore don't wanna be out in the middle of the river and have it bust loose and drop hides an' all into the drink."

Marchand chuckled, picturing Beauchamp splashing in the water, "The Ojibwe people made birchbark canoes and sealed the seams with boiled pine tar. Don't know why that wouldn't work on the boats. Crow's Heart said one bullboat would carry what three horses carries, maybe more. An' if they're tied together, wouldn't hafta have a man in each one and they could haul even more."

"Yeah, an' it'd be easier to build a bullboat than a raft. But that's only if'n we get some buffler," mused Beauchamp. He glanced up and grinned, "You know, them women are prob'ly purty good at skinnin' a buffalo! We could shoot 'em, they could skin 'em, and we could get started on them bullboats and be on the water in no time!"

Marchand nodded his head, grinning as he thought about what he and his two friends had planned about taking over when they were ready to start on the river. With the boats lashed together, maybe a raft in the lead, he and his two friends could handle everything. And they would have the slave to do the work, the women to keep 'em comp'ny, and all the pelts and goods for themselves. Things were beginning to look pretty good after all. He chuckled to himself and knocked the dottle from his pipe as he rose to go to his blankets.

The sky was overcast, low lying clouds obscured the hot sun and the day promised to be a good one for catching up on their sleep. Beauchamp had said that this would be a good day to rest up the horses and get some much-needed sleep themselves, and they would get an early start tomorrow. No one argued or complained, and in short order, snores, snorts and coughs came from the blankets of the men.

Otter and Dove busied themselves cleaning up after the men, taking the tin plates and cups to the creek to scrub with the sand and gravel. As they knelt together, Dove whispered to her sister, "Was that Wolf?"

Otter smiled, nodded, and answered, "I'm sure of it. His cry always had that funny little squeal at the end, it sounded like a whistle," she giggled at the thought.

"But we don't know if Gabe is with him," responded Dove, reaching for a handful of sand to scrub the cups before her.

They spoke in Shoshone, uncertain if anyone was near and wanting to be as cautious as possible. "If my man was not with him, he would come into the camp. But Gabe must have him and they are coming together. But, we still must do what we can," started Otter until she felt a kick at her back. She turned to see a grinning Morgan who said, "Soon. Soon pretty girl, you're gonna be mine," he snarled.

Otter's eyes showed white and her nostrils flared. She gritted her teeth, forcing herself to remain calm and not respond to the disgusting man. She feared him more than the others, even the big man, Beaulieux, was not as bad as this one and if she had a knife she would gut him like buffalo and stuff his innards in his mouth. His kind was the same whether they were white or Indian and would never deserve any mercy, for Otter knew he would show her none. He mumbled, "Soon," and laughed as he turned away to go to his blankets.

26 / Sight

The wet nose of Wolf brought Gabe instantly awake. The black beast gave a slight whimper and trotted to the edge of the trees, looking in the distance at their back trail. Gabe, after his customary look around, rolled from his blankets, rifle in hand and in a crouch went to Wolf's side. Wolf stood, tensed and with his head lowered, growling as he looked at their backtrail. Gabe dropped to one knee, put his hand on Wolf's scruff and asked, "What is it boy, what do you see?" and looked in same direction. At first, he saw nothing. Then a faint wisp of dust rose from beyond the narrow ravine that marked the hanging trail that almost took them to the canyon bottom. It was there, then gone.

He looked a moment longer, then turned back to retrieve his telescope. When he returned to Wolf's side, the black wolf gave only a cursory glance at

Gabe then stared in the distance. Gabe lifted the scope, followed the trail back along the canyon rim and beyond. There, there was more dust then of a sudden the dust came alive with several mounted horses. Gabe stared, shielding the end of the scope with one hand as he rested his elbow on his knee, and watched. They were too far away to identify, but it was a good-sized band and he had no doubt they were Crow, too many for a hunting party but obscured by the dust as they were, he couldn't make out their number.

He turned to look back over his shoulder, wondering just how far behind the raiders he might be and went to the trees, looking for a better promontory to look to the north. He guessed the Crow to be at least seven or eight miles behind him, but it was a rough trail and slow going. He went to a stack of rocks and quickly climbed up to belly down and search the trail to the north, hoping to see some sign of the raiders. He slowly scanned from the visible trail and beyond. To the northeast, a swell of ground showed the tail end of the Absaroka mountains that leveled out into a long series of ridges and flat top mesas.

The river below cut through the end of those mesas to make its way to the flat lands beyond. Directly in front of him the dry country that was scarred by deep gullies and ravines, marked by the burnt umber and orange of the clay soil, stood in stark contrast to the timbered ridges behind him and off his left shoulder. But that was where the raiders had to be. They were following the river and were probably bound for the Missouri River that claimed this north country as its own.

He slowly scanned the countryside with the scope. He paused, thinking he saw a sliver of smoke, searched again and could see nothing. Yet he knew they could be no more than a day, or even less, ahead of him. Now, what should he do about the Crow? Should he try to catch up to the raiders before the Crow? And then what? If the Crow caught the raiders, there was no reason to expect them to treat Ezra and the women any different than the renegades. And did these Indians know that the raiders had been ransacking other Crow villages? Which was something he only knew because of the sign left at the camp, the body with Crow moccasins and scalp.

He turned back to look at the oncoming dust cloud, shook his head and quickly went to Ebony and started saddling the stallion. Wolf stayed at his side and within moments, the three started across the long shoulder of the timber covered ridge, hoping to put some distance between them and the Crow before they saw his sign or dust. His chosen route paralleled the trail below on the flats. There was more cover with the scattered piñon and juniper, but it was still open. His only hope was that the war party would be focused on the trail of the raiders and unconcerned about a single rider high up on the shoulder of the ridge. The soil was more adobe or clay and there were patches of buffalo grass among the clusters of cacti, he glanced over his shoulder to see if he was raising much dust and there was little or none. He nodded to himself and kicked Ebony to a canter, aiming for the distant arroyo where he thought he saw smoke.

He varied the gait from a canter to a walk or trot and back again, wanting to cover as much ground as possible and distance himself from his pursuers. The big ridge to his left bent toward the west and the flat shoulder narrowed, rising up with a barrier of steep basaltic cliffs. Slightly below stood two flat top buttes, with a steep sided ravine dividing the two and snaking its way to the flats below. After over two hours on the trail, Gabe reined up, bent down to pat Ebony on the side of his neck, "So, boy. Which way do we go? Huh?" He glanced at his backtrail, saw nothing, and looked below. They were standing before a slight knob, streaked with a band of white that topped off the burnt umber skirt that trailed to the flats. He stood in his stirrups, saw the sunlight bouncing off something and leaned to the side to see a small natural tank of water below the mound. Beyond the tank, he thought he saw a dim trail that bent around the lower butte and headed into the flatlands.

He gigged Ebony off their point, and he started down the slope. With his hind heels digging into the soft soil, Ebony walked stiff-legged with his front legs as they slid to the bottom of the incline. Gabe reined Ebony to the tank, let him drink, then took to the trail at the foot of the butte. Once on the back side of the butte, he turned back, looked at the flat top and stepped down. He ground tied Ebony, took the scope from the saddle bags and started climbing the back side of the butte, using both hands and feet to crab his way to the top.

He dropped to one knee, pushed his hat back and stretched out the scope, looking at the scarred and rocky terrain between the ridge and the gorge. The narrow trail wound between the ravines, arroyos, rocky outcrops, and narrow defiles, to make its way to the flats just below his butte. He carefully scanned the edge of the gorge and the many ravines that made him picture some giant monster that clawed the land like a dog digging for a bone, but he knew it was the simple formation of time worn terrain marred by the winter run-off and spring floods. Then a puff of dust rose from beyond a deep ravine and he focused in on the spot. The band of Crow rose from the scarred land, still on the trail of the raiders. They had passed the small creek where Gabe had taken to the ridge, obviously following the tracks of the raiders. Still too far away to count, he estimated they were three or more hours behind him.

He turned back to scope the deep arroyo where he thought he saw smoke, walked the scope down the long cut, and stopped. He focused in on a point that appeared to be a low cut, possibly where the trail dropped into the bottom. With the sky overcast and thick with dingy clouds, smoke would be hard to see, but the far edge of that ravine showed dark and he thought he saw a wisp of smoke rising to dissipate among the overcast colors. Maybe.

With a glance over his shoulder, he slipped the scope into its case and started his slipping and sliding down the edge of the butte to Ebony. As he put the scope back in the saddlebags, he lifted his eyes to the sun, used his hands to calculate the remaining daylight, and consider how far he was from the raiders camp, if that was what he saw. *Let's see, it's about two, three hours to that arroyo where they're camped, and the Crow are about that same distance behind. And with no more than three hours daylight left, they won't come on that camp until night. That's if they keep on the trail after dark, so, at the earliest, it won't be till deep dark 'fore they get there. Hmmm . . .* And he began to consider what possibilities he had as he mounted up and pointed Ebony back to the dim trail. It was a trail that appeared to line out toward the distant arroyo, but there was nothing that would offer any cover. The tallest growth was the sage and greasewood that stood no higher than his shoulder or the withers on Ebony, and mighty few of those.

***

Ezra was tied, hands behind the trunk, to the only sizable cottonwood in the ravine bottom. But it was a dead snag, the rough bark had long since dropped to the ground and the smooth trunk was a relief compared to what he had been tied to in other camps. He had already gathered more firewood than what they would need, stacked and restacked the fur bales, tended to the horses and built a lean-to shelter for the women. Morgan and Moreau were more concerned about getting some sleep than finding work for Ezra, so they tied him to the standing cottonwood, gave him a kick for good measure, then went to their blankets.

Ezra leaned back against the snag and thought he felt it move a little. He looked up at the two scraggly branches that stood out like arms on a scarecrow and pushed against the big trunk. It moved just a little. He looked around the camp to see if anyone was watching, then leaned against it again, feeling it give a little and as it did he heard a moan as the trunk or root scraped against a rock or something. He stopped his movement, looking around again. The women were stretched out in their lean-to, apparently asleep. The others were scattered about, each one choosing his spot for shade and comfort and isolation and none standing guard. Beauchamp thought there was nothing or no one to be concerned about and believed no small hunting party would dare attack their well-armed group. No one wanted to stand guard, so no argument was given, each choosing to get some sleep. No one moved, then something caught his eye. Morgan had come from his blankets and gone to the bushes and was returning. He stood looking at the others and Ezra dropped his head as if he were sleeping, but with one eye open a slit, he watched the lone figure standing by the alders where his blankets lay.

Ezra watched as Morgan began picking his way quietly among the sleepers, working closer to the lean-to of the women. Ezra watched, knowing what the man had in mind and his anger rose as he drew his knees to his chest. He steeled himself against the pain, and leaned into the trunk, but waited. When Morgan dropped to his knees beside Dove and reached out, Ezra leaned tight against the smooth trunk, dug his heels in and pushed. He felt it give just a little, and drew his knees back, digging in his heels, just as he heard the growl from Morgan as he put his hand over Dove's mouth.

Ezra dug his heels deep, wiggled his arms and shoulders to move up the trunk, then gave a shove with all his strength. The big muscles bulged against the taut buckskins, his thigh muscles swelled, his back arched and with everything he had, he pushed. He looked high overhead and saw the branches wobble, then the bigger one on the back split with a cracking sound and dropped to the ground, just as the big tree gave way and began to fall. With the weight of one large branch above Ezra's head, it counterbalanced the trunk and the entire thing began to topple, bending Ezra over at the waist. But as the weight of the tree came down, the trunk broke apart, leaving a piece of the trunk still tied to Ezra that hung below his hips, and extended to his shoulders, but it wasn't enough to stop him. In the same instant the tree hit the ground with a crash, Ezra dove toward the lean-to, using the tree trunk as his weapon and struck Morgan in his side, knocking him from Dove and rolling him onto his back beneath Ezra and the stub of the tree.

Ezra drove his knee into Morgan's gut then dropped his shoulder, still bearing the trunk, into the face of the attacker. Ezra struggled to his feet, growling at the downed and injured Morgan, who was grabbing at his belt for a knife, but the scabbard was empty, and he looked with frightened eyes at

Ezra, now standing over him, eyes blazing and lips snarling like a mad dog. Morgan tried to scoot back away, but Ezra lunged at him, lifted his foot and buried it in the man's stomach, bending him in half. Morgan rolled to his side, hands at his stomach as he emptied his guts on the ground.

"Back off!" came the order from Beauchamp, a pistol in his hand threatening.

Ezra looked at the leader, breathed deep with his nostrils flaring, and growled, "He was attackin' the women!"

Beauchamp looked at Morgan, then at the women who were standing beside their lean-to, "Is that right?" he demanded.

Both Dove and Otter nodded then Otter spoke, "He held a knife on me, and his hand on her mouth. He was reaching for her, but she was kicking at him, then Ezra hit him."

Beauchamp looked from the still wallowing Morgan to Marchand, "You better get him under control 'fore I kill him! When he touches those women he's messin' with my payday, and don't forget that!"

Moreau was standing beside Marchand and pointed at Ezra, "Did you see that? He uprooted that whole tree!"

"Ummhumm, and you would do well to remember that. Even tied up, he's dangerous," answered

Marchand, turning back to his blankets, hoping he could go back to sleep, but knowing it wouldn't happen. He called over his shoulder, "Just lay him on his side an' tie his feet to his hands. That'll keep him from anything."

Dove started to go to Ezra, but was warned off by Moreau, then on second thought he ordered, "You! You get him loose from that tree then we'll re-tie him yonder."

Dove nodded and went to Ezra, who looked down and asked, "Are you all right?"

"Yes. You hit him before he could do anything." She turned to glance back at Moreau, then busied herself with Ezra's bonds at his back, urged him to sit down so the trunk could be moved, and as she worked, she whispered, "Otter has the knife that man used. She hid it in our blankets."

27 / Stalk

It was dry country and he didn't want to push Ebony any more than absolutely necessary. The flat stretched out before him like an empty table top, broken only by clumps of prickly pear and the occasional cholla. Some of the skeletal cacti were barren but an occasional clump still showed the bright pink blossoms so common in the spring that contrasted with the barrenness of the desert-like flats. Puffs of dust obscured the hooves of the big black and his coat that usually had a deep sheen was now dimmed with the heavy powder. Gabe doffed his hat and beat at his arms, chest, and legs, to rid himself of the layer of dust. Although it seemed further, he had ridden about five miles when the desert was scarred by a long and deep ravine that blocked his way, but the ancient trail he followed bent over the edge and took them into the shady bottom, giving a brief but welcome respite from the hot sun. Wolf was already at the water, lapping it up and glancing around before dipping his muzzle again. The usually black wolf now appeared dun colored, until he rolled in the grass and shook violently.

Gabe had stepped down and dropped the reins to allow Ebony to drink his fill and once the big black was satisfied Gabe stripped off the saddle and let the big horse mimic Wolfand have a good roll in the grass. Once Ebony stood and looked around then Gabe let the animals stand watch and he stuck his face in the cool water, splashed it on his neck and ran his wet fingers through his hair and whiskers. He took a couple handfuls and splashed the back of his neck and let it run down his back and did the same with his chest. He considered a roll in the grass but knew it wouldn't do any good, what he needed was a good long bath in the cold water of a deep river. But that would have to wait.

He lifted his eyes to the setting sun that seemed to stand as a lone beacon at the head of the long ravine and knew this ravine and stop was a fortuitous one. He was considering his options regarding approaching the raiders. He contemplated just riding into their camp but knew the men that tried to kill him would probably recognize him and want to finish the job, so he ruled that out. But the terrain that held the trail offered no cover and would prevent any approach from the flats. But now, this ravine would take him further west, where he could cross over to the coulee where the camp of the raiders lay, and perhaps make a stealthy attack from the shelter of the brush in the coulee. He grinned at the thought and snatched up the reins, saddled the black and mounted up. The sun was resting atop the long mesas north of the timber covered ridge he had followed earlier, and dusk would allow him enough light to get closer.

He rode into the sun, following the ravine that carried the little stream, but it soon forked, and he took the dry creek bottom that bent to the northwest. Although he was riding toward the end of the long ridge, he would turn to the north and the wider coulee soon. But the dry creek bent to the north and joined another broad gully that pointed north. Gabe grinned, thinking, *This couldn't have been better if I designed it myself!* The new gully soon widened, showing itself to be a dry bed of a much larger watershed that came from the higher mountains, but was void of water now, save a few small pools tucked under some thin willows. As he rode the bottom, he saw the east shoulder of the arroyo to be a long flat mesa, marked by abutments of orange and white that caught the bright colors of the sunset and held them as if sapping the colors into their hillsides. When the arroyo fed into the larger coulee, Gabe reined up and stepped down. The dim light of dusk was fading, and he had to prepare himself for the plan he formulated as he rode.

His hand went to the bandage at his head, slowly removed it and felt the wound. It was dry and scabby, the only moisture in his hair was from sweat. He checked the poultice at his hip, removed it and felt the scab and believed it was healing well. For now, he chose to leave the poultice at the deeper knife wound at his back, but he arched his back then moved his arms and shoulders to loosen the muscles and see how the wound might hinder him, but he was satisfied and began stripping the saddle from Ebony.

He busied himself cleaning all his weapons. With so much time on the dusty trails, they were in need of a good cleaning and he left nothing untouched. As he worked, he calculated. He estimated he was about two miles above their camp, providing their camp was where he expected it to be, and it would take less than an hour to get there, but as he drew near he would have to be stealthy and that would take time. Once he was within two to three hundred yards, he would go to ground and the going would be slow. If the war party of Crow chose to make an attack at night, the earliest he expected that, would be about midnight, or maybe a little earlier.

He looked at Wolf, lying by his feet, and grinned, "You comin' with me Wolf?" Then he thought it might not be a good idea, the young wolf might rush up to Otter or Dove and wake some of the men. But, having him along gave him another pair of eyes that might help.

Gabe finished cleaning the weapons, and began loading each one, debating about what he wanted to take with him on this foray. He opted to leave the Ferguson behind, taking his Mongol bow and quiver of arrows, and both saddle pistols and the Bailes over/under in his belt. He hoped he could free Ezra and give him a pistol, and maybe one to Otter, but . . . he tried to picture what was about to happen, but shook his head, unknowing.

***

The *Apsáalooke* band was made up of warriors of the *Ashalaho*, or Mountain Crow, led by Chief No Intestines and his War Leader, Long Hair, and warriors of the *Apsáalooke* or River Crow, led by Chief Red Calf and his War Leader, Spotted Crow. It was No Intestines's villages that had been raided by the whites as they traveled upstream of the Yellowstone before crossing south to the Shoshone River. The Mountain Crow had mounted a war party of fifteen warriors to accompany their chief as they pursued the raiders and were joined by the River Crow when the single survivor of the encounter with the lone white man and his black wolf returned to the village to tell of the mighty white warrior who had killed four of his fellow warriors. Now the band numbered thirty-two battle tested warriors of the Crow people, or *Apsáalooke*, bent on retribution and elimination of these white men that would slaughter their people and ransack the villages.

White Goose and Strikes Twice, the scouts sent to trail the raiders and the lone white man, rode back to the band to report. It was late afternoon and the sun was glaring brightly from beneath the heavy cloud cover, making its way to the western mountains when the band stopped for water and food at the wide arroyo known as Deadman's Creek. Strikes Twice spoke first, "The lone man with the wolf was trailing the others but turned away to the mountains." He pointed up the same ravine where the band now rested.

"He is the same one that killed your brothers?" asked Spotted Crow.

"Yes. He rides a great black horse and the wolf goes with him. He is the one."

White Goose added, "The raiders are camped in the next valley. They did not travel this day. They have two women, Shoshone, as captives, and a man that looks like the buffalo. They are afraid of the buffalo man and keep him bound."

Both chiefs and war leaders sat against the ravine bank, listening to the report of the scouts. Chief No

Intestines looked at the setting sun, "The valley of their camp is two fingers away," referring to the time it takes the sun to travel the width of two fingers, "We cannot be there and attack before dark. We could take them at night, or . . . at first light."

Red Calf nodded, looked at Spotted Crow and then to Long Hair, "By first light, we could be in place and take them with little fight. They have many guns and if would be good to take them by surprise before they come from their blankets."

Spotted Crow nodded, "It is good."

"They have ridden at night and could again," stated Long Hair. These were the war leaders that spoke and had led many raids against their enemies and on other tribes to take horses and more.

"Then we will send scouts to watch. If they start to leave, they can signal with a fire," offered No Intestines.

The others nodded their agreement and with a wave of his hand, the chief sent the scouts back to watch the raiders.

As they did on their first scout, the two men followed the contour of the land, moving below a table top lift that overshadowed a dry wash that angled toward the bigger coulee with the camp of the raiders. Dusk had dropped the curtain of darkness over the land, but the sky was clearing, and the big moon was showing as a glow behind the thin layer of clouds. If the wind continued, the clouds would soon lift and give the waning moon its chance to shine.

The two scouts tethered their horses to a clump of greasewood and followed the long slanting mesa top to the edge that stood over the break in the coulee wall. By line of sight, they were just over half a mile from the camp, but the winking lights of the campfire told of the presence of the raiders. But the fire soon dimmed, and the scouts decided to retrieve their horses and move closer. To the left of the cut that carried the trail to the bottom, the mesa ended in a layer of basaltic rimrock, but the flattop was about two hundred fifty feet above the valley floor, giving the scouts a clear view of the entire camp.

With their horses staked out well back from the edge, Strikes Twice led the way, dropping to a crouch as he neared the edge, then went to his belly. White Goose bellied up beside his friend, as they rested their chins on the back of their folded hands and watched. Even with eyes accustomed to the dark, the figures below were in the shadows and were indistinct at best. But the horses were easily seen as they were picketed in two lines that cordoned off the camp except where the trees were thickest.

The creek in the bottom carried little runoff water but pooled often in the shallows of sharp bends. Called Dry Head Creek, before the month was through it would be dry, and what greenery it now held would wither away as well. But the horses had their fill and most now stood hipshot as the men and women below went to their blankets. Strikes Twice rolled to his back, cupped his hands behind his head and whispered to White Goose, "You watch, I sleep. Wake me later."

28 / Strike

"Big Devil, you take first watch, Crow's Heart, you take second, Marchand'll take third and I'll take the last watch," instructed Beauchamp as the men stood from the fire and turned toward their blankets. Marchand looked at him, "What about those two?" nodding toward Morgan and Moreau.

"I don't trust 'em with the women, do you?" growled a tired Beauchamp, anxious to get to his blankets.

"No, s'pose not. But they're gonna have to take a turn sometime!" compromised Marchand, turning away and starting to the tree line where he had prepared his sleeping spot. The others went to their places, Big Devil mumbling as he walked to the opening at the end of the picket lines. A big ponderosa stood as a lone landmark that would serve as cover and something to lean against. He knew enough not to expose his silhouette even in the darkness, but he didn't expect anyone to approach their camp, even if they knew there were only six men, not counting the captives.

Big Devil had seldom known fear and enjoyed a good fight. He had claimed many honors among his people as a warrior and was held in high esteem, until he killed that squaw. She was the woman of their war leader and had teased him and taunted him until he could stand it no longer and he caught her, took her to the trees, and was going to teach her what a great warrior he was until her man and his brothers came after them. He was forced to leave the village, was banished from the tribe, and thought himself lucky when he joined these raiders.

He walked along the picket line of horses, touching several, letting them know he was near, but the horses knew him and were unconcerned. When he reached the end of the second picket line, he turned back and went to his chosen place at the foot of the ponderosa. He leaned back against the tree, felt some sap sticking to his tunic, twisted around to a better and more comfortable position, although the tree was between him and the campers, but his concern was for the valley and hillsides away from the camp. He bent down to look from under the branches at the moon, saw nothing but the glow behind the clouds and leaned back, wiggling his rump into the long dry needles for some comfort and relaxed.

***

When Gabe was ready to start, darkness had blanketed the land for two hours, and with a glance to the glow of the moon that was still trying to pierce the remaining clouds, he started down the coulee. With his eyes well accustomed to the dark, he broke into a trot, staying in the grass, moving as silently as a puma. In his belt were the two saddle pistols and his Bailes over/under. Each weapon had two barrels and the saddle pistols he had double-shotted to increase the kill power. He didn't expect to do any long-range shooting, although the big pistols were more accurate than most. It was a load at his belt, but necessary. His quiver hung at his hip, his Mongol bow in his hand and he moved easily through the darkness.

As he drew near, the trees showed as tall shadows and he dropped to one knee beside a chokecherry bush. He waited a moment to catch his wind, surveying the valley bottom as best he could in the dim light. He glanced at the glow of the moon and saw the last of the clouds slowly moving and the edge of the moon beginning to show itself. He would be able to see better, but so would they and he preferred the anonymity of the darkness. He waited, watching, glancing at the moon and the clouds. As he watched, the narrow strip of moonlight walked down the draw and hung over the edge of the camp, just for a moment. But it was long enough for him to see the picket lines of the horses, and a quick glimpse of what appeared to be a man on guard at the end of the pickets. Then the break in the clouds closed as another bigger cloud masked the night light, giving Gabe the darkness he wanted.

He crossed the narrow creek, then moved beside the line of brush that bordered the bank away from the camp. He calculated the brush line would take him to the thicker trees where the camp was nestled, and he could approach the camp through the woods and away from the guard. He had been moving on hands and knees, his bow on his back, but as he drew within a stone's throw, he went to his belly. With the tail of his tunic protecting the pistols at his belt, he inched his way forward, careful to avoid any overhanging branches that would brush against his buckskins. When he came in line with the guard, even though he was across the creek and over fifty feet away, Gabe knew any man of the wilderness could see in this dim light and would be wary of any movement. Wolf was belly down beside him, tongue lolling, watching every move and staying close beside him.

The wispy clouds moved, dimpling the area with patches of moonlight, shadowing others. Where the guard sat, the overhanging branches were sparse, and he chose that spot for comfort and the openness to see around him. A patch of dim blue moonlight rested on the man's legs, showing his position clearly to Gabe. The big Indian, over confident in his size to meet any challenge, sat unconcerned and dozing as he wiggled his big form into the bedding of the long needles of the ponderosa.

Gabe looked at the guard, then to the sleeping forms closer to the trees and beyond the picket lines of the horses. As he scanned the horses, he saw the familiar markings on the bay gelding of Ezra, then the blue roan of Otter standing beside the buckskin of Dove. The sorrel was next to the two mustangs, and the packs and saddles were stacked next to the trees. It was always the practice to picket horses beside those that were familiar, giving all the security of familiarity and Gabe considered what he faced. If he was able to free Ezra and the women, they still needed horses and with the guard nearby, that would be difficult at best.

He glanced at the guard again and he seemed to be slumping even more, probably asleep. Gabe brought his bow up, nocking an arrow, then came to one knee as he brought the bow to full draw, he breathed easy, knowing everything depended on this first move. He breathed deep as he sighted down the shaft of the arrow, then let it fly. The slight twang of the bowstring brought the guard instantly awake, but he did not move, and the arrow took him at the base of his neck and pinned him to the tree. The big man choked and grabbed at the shaft, breaking it off at his chest, leaving a short stub protruding as he gagged, kicked with one foot, then sagged in death. He was pinned to the tree and did not slump over, making it appear he was still awake and watching.

Gabe had dropped to one knee beside the willows, watching the camp to see if the choking sounds of the man had alerted either the raiders or the horses, but nothing showed alarm. He dropped down and continued his stealthy approach of the tree line and the camp beyond. Once he was at the end of the picket line close to the trees, he crossed over the stream to approach the horses. He knew they had already caught his smell, but the animals were always wary of dark forms moving in the night. He wanted to make them aware of his presence so they would not spook and alert the others. He spoke softly, hand outstretched, as he neared the blue roan of Otter, and the horses that had their heads lifted and ears pricked, now lowered their heads and relaxed. He moved among them, keeping the horses between him and the sleeping raiders. Once the string of horses had relaxed, he moved back to the edge of the trees and dropped to his knees, then began working his way to the far end of the camp where he expected to find Ezra and the women.

He stayed close to the creek, letting the continual chuckling of the shallow waters cascading over the rocks and rapids to shield any inadvertent sounds he might make. Within moments, he neared the end of the clearing and he moved as silent as a shadow close to the edge. He paused, rose to his feet beside a cluster of skinny aspen, and surveyed the camp. He saw the form of Ezra, lying on his side, hands tied to his feet behind his back. Closer to him was the lean-to, and the blankets that covered the legs of the women were recognized by Gabe to be those of the women and he assumed the dark figures in the lean-to were those of the women. Less than eight feet beyond, were two prone figures, less than two feet apart. Two men were beyond Ezra, about a dozen feet away from him. But Gabe was certain there were more, with the one Indian as a guard, there had to be at least one more, the one that had thrown the knife that took him in the back.

He waited, watching, searching the trees for any sign of others. He knew there were those that always sought solitude, keeping to themselves, avoiding others as much as possible, and he knew that many natives were of that sort, depending only on themselves. Among white men, there are those that work hard, seeking to fulfill their goals and ambitions by their own efforts, depending on no one but themselves, and others who prefer to take what they want from others, refusing to abide by the unwritten codes of morality, decency, and honesty. Those are the ones that will seek refuge in bands of others of like ilk and ambitions and care not with whom they keep company. It was the loner he was concerned with, the type that would be off by themselves, unseen and hidden by the trees, that could prevent Gabe from freeing his friends. He visually searched every break in the trees, every possible trail that led from the clearing, every bit of cover that offered refuge and saw nothing, until a low growl came from beside him and Wolf, standing, his head down, eyes blazing orange in the darkness, teeth showing and slobbers dripping and he took a single step in the direction of the trees beyond the two sleeping forms past Ezra. Movement!

Gabe turned away, facing into the thicker trees and with one hand cupped at his mouth, he let out the peent – peent cry of the nighthawk. He looked back at the moving figure in the trees, saw him stop and turn in his direction. Then a quick glance down at Ezra showed him lifting his head, staring into the darkness. He had recognized the signal he and Gabe had used many times before, but he also knew Gabe was so skilled at giving the call, it was almost impossible to detect it was not from a nighthawk. Gabe slipped the Flemish knife from the sheath at his back, threw it where it stuck within reach of Ezra's hands and watched at his friend twisted around to take the knife and begin working on his bonds.

Gabe had an arrow nocked and watched as the man in the woods moved again. If he was going to relieve the guard, they had only a few moments until the dead guard was discovered. When the shadowy figure continued his move, it was obvious he was going to replace the guard. As soon as he turned away from where Gabe stood, Gabe moved quickly to the side of the women. He dropped to one knee, reached to put a hand on Otter's mouth, but she lifted her hand to stop him. He grinned in the darkness, slipped one of the pistols to her, and whispered for her to waken Dove and follow him.

He started for the trees, stopped beside Ezra and used his smaller knife to finish cutting his friends bonds. Ezra rubbed his wrists, started to rise, when one of the two men beyond the women's lean-to, sat up and hollered. "Get them! They're escaping!" and grabbed for his rifle at his side, but before he could reach his weapon, an arrow pierced his chest. Gabe turned to Otter and Dove, "To the horses!" and nodded in the direction of the picket line.

Gabe tossed the second saddle pistol to Ezra and the man stumbled to his feet. He was nocking another arrow as he stepped beside a nearby tree, blending with the shadow as he searched the camp for the movements of the others. A rifle barked and he heard the whoosh of a lead ball passing within inches of his head and he turned to the two that lay beyond Ezra. He lifted his bow, but the pistol in the hand of Ezra bucked, spat smoke and lead, and the figure that was wrestling with his rifle to reload, groaned as they heard the impact of the two bullets from the double-shotted pistol, and he stumbled backwards, dropping his rifle and as his knees buckled, he fell backwards, his legs kicking out awkwardly, and a choking, gurgling sound coming from his lips.

High on the plateau above the camp, the first shot brought Strikes Twice instantly awake and he rolled over to look below. The darkness showed nothing but the flare of a second blast, then a third. The two scouts saw by the fire of the weapons, that the two figures were shooting at each other. They glanced at one another then back to the camp below. Strikes Twice said, "They are killing each other, or someone has attacked them."

Then a sudden realization prompted Strikes Twice to look at his friend, White Goose, "It is the lone man, the one with the wolf. He has attacked them!" Then he looked at the camp again, trying to see who was shooting. But the darkness hid them from view, and they could see nothing, not even movement.

29 / Flight

The first shot that barely missed Gabe came from the rifle in the hands of Moreau and Gabe's arrow had ended his fight. The second blast was from Marchand, and Ezra's pistol had taken his life, but the rifle ball had cut the shoulder of Ezra, dropping him to one knee as he put his free hand to his shoulder, staying the flow of blood from the wound.

"Whoever you are, I'm gonna gut'chu, then I'm gonna get those women an' use 'em and make 'em take care of me like I deserve!" It was Morgan, trying to make Gabe reveal his location, but Gabe knew his intent, and knew that from his place beyond the lean-to, that the black forest behind him obscured his position from the braggart and Gabe did not respond. "Did you hear me! I'm gonna use those women!" he screamed, desperate for a target.

Gabe had an arrow knocked, and stood ready, but

the same darkness that shielded him, hid the image of Morgan and the man was smart enough to not move. Gabe did not realize that Wolf was no longer at his side, but stood waiting and watching, trusting Ezra to watch the one man on that side of the camp. For several moments, the camp was silent, no one moved, no one spoke, even the night sounds were silenced.

Then a voice came from the darkness behind Morgan, "You will not use me!" It was Otter, she was behind the man, but Gabe could not see her and could not risk a shot from his bow. An arrow, once loosed, was mindless and did only as bidden by the archer, and Otter was too important to risk as a target.

Morgan had spun around, looking for the source of the remark, but the blackness of the woods was now in favor of the women, while Morgan was silhouetted as he stood away from the trees with only the clearing behind him and the dim light of the moon stretching vague shadows. He frantically searched for movement, holding his rifle at his shoulder, snatching short breaths, twisting, searching, desperate.

Otter knew she had the advantage but was determined to make her tormentor feel the same fear he had forced upon her. She cocked the second hammer of the pistol and quickly stepped aside from the sound that racketed across the clearing. He fired at what he thought was the figure of the woman, but her voice came from another position. "That was not me. Are you afraid white man?" She quickly moved back to her first position, watching the man fumble with his rifle and powder horn, "You are about to die white man," she added, continuing to move. Morgan grabbed at his tomahawk, threw it at the shadow, but it whispered past and landed in the brush beyond. "Are you ready?" asked Otter, moving again. Then Morgan, slipped his ramrod from the barrel and started to bring the rifle to his shoulder when he saw the blossom of orange and grey as the pistol bucked in the hands of the woman.

The double-shotted blast took Morgan in the upper chest, knocking him backwards a step and as he struggled, he dropped his rifle, clutching his chest and Otter stepped closer, glaring at the man that had taunted and tormented her. She lifted the pistol and Morgan said, "You only had one shot and it didn't kill me!" he forced a chuckle as he stumbled again. He saw the pistol in the light of the moon, saw the hammer fall, the flare of powder igniting in the pan, the blast of fire and smoke from the end of the barrel and he thought he saw the balls explode through the grey cloud of gunsmoke, then felt the impact of two lead balls. He thought, Two balls? But she only had one shot, and one . . . he dropped to his knees, both hands at his chest. He felt the warmth of his blood flowing over his hands, and started to look down, but darkness closed over his eyes, and his last thought was Nooo. . . and he fell on his face.

Gabe looked at Ezra, "Can you make it to the horses?"

"Watch me!" he declared and took to the trees.

Gabe watched the clearing, remembering there was another man that was on the far side of Ezra, and the man in the trees. He was certain the one in the trees was the Indian that had attacked him when he had downed the elk. But now, nothing moved, no sound came from the trees and the darkness. He slowly backed deeper into the trees, then moved quickly and quietly toward the picket line. He saw Otter and Dove saddling their horses, while Ezra watched the camp, pistol at the ready. Gabe came close, "Do you know where your weapons are?"

"Yeah, they were with the packs. You watch, I'll find 'em," answered Ezra, sticking the pistol in his belt. Then Gabe remembered Wolf, and looked around for the beast, but saw nothing. Ezra dug through the packs, searching for their weapons, found the rifles and his warclub, but not his knives, tomahawk, and pistol. He came to Gabe's side, "Can't find my belt weapons. I think that one that Otter killed had 'em. I'm gonna go check his bedroll."

Gabe responded by handing him his powder horn and possibles pouch, "Reload first."

Ezra nodded, reloading the first barrel of the saddle pistol, knowing the second still held Gabe's original load. Gabe suggested, "I double-shotted 'em, you might wanna do the same."

Ezra nodded, did as suggested, then started back to the bodies of the two men that had been his guards and tormentors. Within moments, he returned, weapons in hand, grinning. The women had finished gearing up the horses, including loading the panniers and parfleches for the packhorses. Otter spoke softly, "We are ready."

Above the rimrock, Strikes Twice, jumped up and said over his shoulder, "I will start the fire!"

White Goose remained prone, watching the shadowy figures below. There was a short pause and then another shot, followed shortly by another. He rolled to his side, "They are still shooting. I think they will all be dead when our people come."

"But Red Calf will still want to see and if there are more, then we will take them."

Gabe nodded to Otter, back stepped toward the horses, then led the way afoot and at a trot. He splashed across the creek and started upstream toward where he left Ebony and his gear. From the shadows came the wolf, trotting alongside as if they were just out for a stretch. A short time later, Gabe dropped to a walk, but kept a quick pace and the group soon arrived at the side of Ebony, who lifted his head with a low whinny as they neared.

Gabe snatched the rein from the brush and swung aboard the big black, then Ezra spoke, "You know, we could just camp here an' wait till daylight to leave. Where we goin' anyway?"

Gabe chuckled, "I figgered we'd find us a tradin' post somewhere and re-supply. I wanted to get a letter off to my sister and the lawyer my dad chose, been thinkin' 'bout some things. As for stayin' around, well, how many of those fellas are still kickin'?"

Ezra thought for a moment, "Well, there's the Mandan scout, the Assiniboine known as Big Devil," he paused as Gabe frowned, then questioned.

"Big Devil? Was he a big man, Indian, buckskins?"

"Uh, yeah. You see him?"

"Yeah, but the last time I saw him he was just hangin' out by a big tree by that other picket line," drawled Gabe. "Anybody else?"

Ezra frowned at Gabe's answer, not understanding, but added, "Yeah, the one man that was the leader of the bunch. He was known as Beauchamp. I think he ducked into the woods after I shot the one that clipped me."

"That means there's two; the Mandan and Beauchamp," replied Gabe.

"Sounds right."

Gabe chuckled again, "Well, I think they're gonna have some visitors. About twenty or more mad Crow that's been followin' 'em."

Ebony suddenly lifted his head, ears pricked, and looked at the mouth of the draw that held the dry creek bed. Wolf came to his feet, a low growl sounding, and several mounted warriors appeared before them. Gabe saw four riding side by side directly toward them, then four more that came from the far side of the small creek, rising up from the willows, and four more that came over the edge of the ravine. Gabe lifted his hand to his friends, signaling them to not make any moves. They were surrounded and if they chose to fight it out, it would be costly.

One warrior came forward, looked directly at Gabe, then a quick glance at the big stallion and his eyes dropped to the black wolf, still in his attack stance, teeth showing and eyes glaring. Gabe spoke softly to Wolf, "Easy boy," and the wolf took one step back, relaxed but did not take his eyes off the leader.

"I am Spotted Crow of the *Binnéessiippeele Apsáalooke.* You are the man with the black wolf that killed our warriors," stated the war leader, speaking in his own tongue, but using sign language as well.

Gabe nodded, answered in English and sign, "I am known as Spirit Bear. Your warriors attacked me and I fought them. They were brave men and died honorably. But I also spared one man," Gabe had recognized the man beside Spotted Crow with the bandage on his upper arm, and pointed toward him with his chin, "for him to tell you the truth of the fight. I did not want to kill your warriors, but I did not want to die." He motioned toward his friends, "Your enemies, the white men, raiders, had taken our women and my friend, Black Buffalo. We have killed many and taken only what was ours. There are horses and packs that bear the goods taken from your people," he nodded toward the camp, "and there is at least one man, maybe two, that are still alive."

Spotted Crow looked long at Gabe, then at the packhorses and the others. With another glance at Gabe, he gigged his horse toward Ezra and stopped beside him. He reached out for Ezra's hand, and after a pause, Ezra surrendered it to the war leader who examined the wounds to his wrists. He looked at Ezra, asked, "Did you kill the one who did this?"

Ezra let a slow grin split his face, and answered, "I killed one," then nodded toward Otter, "She killed one."

Spotted Crow frowned, looked at Otter, then back to Ezra, "She killed one?"

"Yes. He said he would hurt her, so she killed him. Before that she gutted another man that tried to hurt her."

Spotted Crow scowled, looked from Ezra to Otter

who sat stoically, waiting. The war leader reined his horse around to go to Gabe and asked, "Is she your woman?" nodding toward Otter.

Gabe grinned, "Yes."

"Is it safe to sleep beside her?" he asked.

Gabe chuckled, "I sleep lightly."

Spotted Crow chuckled. Then with a more sober expression, "The Shoshone have been friends of the *Apsáalooke*, you have killed enemies of the *Apsáalooke*, you are now friends with the *Apsáalooke*." With a wave of his hand, the twelve warriors rode away, going downstream toward the camp of the raiders.

Gabe looked at Otter and then at Ezra and Dove, he chuckled, "Let's put some distance between them and us 'fore he changes his mind!"

"I'm for that!" answered Ezra, chuckling.

Otter reined up beside her man, smiling, and said, "You only sleep lightly because you snore so happily!"

30 / Escape

Jacques Beauchamp crouched behind the big ponderosa that held the body of Big Devil, watching Gabe, Ezra and the women gear up their animals. The big white man and the slave had killed his men and now were taking some of his plunder and horses, he gritted his teeth, forcing himself to stay hidden, although he wanted to shoot that impudent negra and take those women, but his one shot with his rifle would do nothing more than let them know where he was hidden. He didn't know that Crow's Heart stood behind him, watching the others prepare to leave.

When the black man went to the trees, Beauchamp thought to follow, but reconsidered when he turned and was face to face with the Mandan. Crow's Heart glared at Beauchamp, his look pinning him in place as he whispered, "We get them later. Many *Apsáalooke* come!" he nodded to the butte above the camp.

Beauchamp watched as Ezra returned and spoke to the other man. They mounted up, taking the three packhorses and gear that was theirs, and rode upstream on the small creek. Once they were beyond the brush, Beauchamp looked at the Mandan, "We got time to get our horses an' some o' them pelts?"

The scout nodded, started for his own horse, but Beauchamp implored him to help load the best bundles of pelts on the pack horses. Once those were secure, they hurriedly saddled their own horses and within moments were on the run down the coulee to make their escape.

When the signal fire flared up, Strikes Twice and White Goose swung aboard their horses and took off at a run to meet up with the rest of the war party. When they came to the band, White Goose reported, "They fighting themselves. Several shots, too dark to see."

Strikes Twice added, "I believe it was the warrior with the wolf that attacked them."

The two chiefs and their war leaders listened, then Chief No Intestines ordered, "You," nodding to Chief Red Calf and his war leader, Spotted Crow, "take your warriors to the draw upstream of the camp, we will strike from below."

It was a simple plan and the chief of the Mountain Crow had confidence in his fellow chief to mount the attack wisely. He trusted Red Calf and knew they would box off the wide gulley and prevent anyone escaping to the west. It was No Intestine's responsibility to make a direct attack on the camp and box them off on the east end of the ravine. But in the darkness, nothing is certain, and anything could happen. He watched as Red Calf led his warriors across the flat toward the upper end of the coulee then kneed his horse forward.

With his war leader, Long Hair, whose name in the Crow language was *Itchuuwaaóoshbishish* or Red Plume at the Temple, at his side, Chief No Intestines suggested, "It would be wise for you to take as many warriors as you need and cross the ravine below the camp and come at them from the far side. We will attack into the draw at the cut."

Long Hair nodded, reined his mount to the side and picked seven warriors to follow him into the lower end of the draw. The chief had reined up and watched his war leader start for the draw at a canter, his men following. He motioned for White Goose to come alongside and gigged his horse forward to make their way to the cut in the draw. He looked at the scout, "How many?"

White Goose answered, "We saw four white men, two women captive, the buffalo man captive, and a big warrior, not Crow or Shoshone, and a Mandan scout."

"Will the captives fight?"

"The buffalo man was tied to a tree; the women had no weapons."

The chief nodded, dismissed the scout with a wave, and kicked his horse to a canter. When they were within about a hundred yards of the cut, the chief stopped and turned to face his warriors. He spoke quietly as he ordered White Goose to lead the first bunch of five warriors into the cut. "Go quietly until you are seen, then fight. We," nodding to the eight warriors behind him, "will come after. Long Hair will attack when he sees you."

White Goose nodded, excited about his first chance to lead an attack, but did his best to be reserved and composed. He motioned to the warriors to the right of the chief, reined his horse around and started to the cut at a walk, all the while readying his weapons. He would use his bow first, yet his lance was carried in a loop of braided rawhide at his horse's flank and ready at hand. He fingered his tomahawk, knife, and reached down to touch his war shield. He initially thought to keep his bow-holding arm free, but then decided to use the shield. He slipped it onto his left arm, then picked up his bow, nocked an arrow, and watched as they neared the cut that broke into the wider ravine that held the camp. He glanced to the left to the smoldering signal fire, then focused on the attack.

In his eagerness, White Goose kicked his horse into a run as the cut opened into the valley. The warriors followed his lead and the six men charged into the camp screaming their war cries, searching for a target for their wrath. But there was nothing, no one stood to defend themselves, no shots were fired, but White Goose saw the bodies scattered. He jumped to the ground and ran to the body of Marchand, shot an arrow into it, and dropped to one knee, drawing his knife to take a scalp. The other warriors found the bodies of Morgan and Moreau, and one man pierced the body of Morgan with his lance, then dropped to the ground and turned, tomahawk raised and fell on the body, angered that the man was already dead. The warriors were screaming their war cries, but there was no one left alive. They kicked at the bodies, scalped them, and began mutilating each one.

Long Hair and his warriors charged into the camp, reining their horses around, and several went to the still picketed horses, now skittish and pulling at their tethers. Within moments, all the warriors of Chief No Intestines were scrambling through the camp, snatching up rifles, pistols, knives and hawks. Others went to the bundles of pelts and packs of plunder and began rummaging through the remains.

The camp had been pillaged and bodies mutilated when Red Calf and Spotted Crow and their warriors rode into the clearing. Red Calf went to No Intestines and asked, "Were there any left alive?"

"None."

"We found the warrior with the wolf. He had attacked the camp and taken his friend, the buffalo man, and their women, the Shoshone. They took what was theirs and left the rest for our people. They said there were two others left alive, the leader white man, and the Mandan scout."

The River Crow Chief's eyes flared, then he looked at his war leader, Long Hair. "There were two that escaped!"

Spotted Crow stepped forward, "I will take four warriors and go after those."

The two chiefs looked at one another and Red Calf said, "There are horses and goods here for these," nodding to the warriors that had plundered the camp, "and to send more than that after two men and a few pelts is foolish. If they will go, let them go."

"What Red Calf says is wise. My people have suffered enough, and we have far to go to return to our lodges. If your warriors will get vengeance, so be it." He turned to Spotted Crow, "Choose your warriors."

Spotted Crow looked at the men who had followed him and Red Calf from their village and he chose Strikes Twice, White Goose, and two other proven warriors that he had ridden with before, both were young warriors, *Arapoosh* or Sore Belly, and

Chíschipaaliash or Rotten Tail.

They rode into the rising sun as they left the others behind. Spotted Crow and Rotten Tail rode side by side, the others following, as Rotten Tail leaned over to check the tracks of the two men and two packhorses that had fled the camp. The churned trail showed they left at a run, but soon dropped their horses to a trot. Tail looked at Crow, "We will catch them before dark. Their horses will soon tire and they must stop."

"That is hard country, rough trail, slow," answered Crow, knowing the country that bordered the last canyon of the river. Spotted Crow fingered the feathers that hung over his bone breast plate, the eagle was his *Xapáaliia* or Spirit guide and the source of his *Baaxpée*, or power from God. He muttered a silent prayer for the power needed for this quest for vengeance and gigged his horse to a trot.

31 / Reprisal

Gabe and company rode into the dim light of the waning moon. The cloud cover thinned, and the plains were flat, flat except for a deep scar made by spring runoff as it cut its way to the river canyon. They dipped into and out of the steep sided ravine and were bearing due east when the thin line of grey crowded its way at the edge of darkness in the east. The moon was dropping in the west, but the band of grey light widened, the sky showed a dull blue and the eastern horizon was painted with brilliant pink and reds. With greater light, Gabe angled toward the northeast and a cluster of ragged mountains that seemed to stand alone on the edge of the plains. Always one for high ground, he suggested, "Let's head for them mountains yonder and have us a bite to eat. I ain't had a good meal since we parted comp'ny." He looked at Otter, grinning.

"I gathered some of the pickin's we had for the others. We can take time for a good meal," answered Otter, glad to be with her man as she reached for his hand. He stretched across the space between them and grabbed her hand, drawing Ebony closer to her blue roan, and they rode side by side, legs touching, and hands clasped. The little sorrel tugged at the lead rope but followed along.

Ezra and Dove were close, Dove holding Ezra's hand as she applied a poultice of sage and aspen buds while they rode. It would be some time before his raw wrists and ankles healed, but it was a healing time they would both enjoy. It was about two hours after first light when they stopped at the foot of what Gabe had called mountains but were nothing more than ragged ridges that stood about five hundred feet above the plains. They crossed a small arroyo and rode up a shoulder that held a green basin of tall grass and stopped for their meal. Gabe took his scope and started up the ridge while Dove and Ezra gathered some dry wood for the fire and Otter gathered up the fixin's.

With the remainder of the venison in Gabe's pack, some of the turnips and onions from their supply, the women soon had the strip steaks broiling over the flames of the small and smokeless fire and had pushed the turnips and onions into the coals. Ezra looked to the ridge for any sign of Gabe's return and said, "I'm goin' up there to see what he sees."

The women nodded, smiling, knowing the men had missed the company of each other and needed the 'man-time' together. He climbed the steep hillside and dropped to one knee beside his friend who had shielded himself behind a stack of flat granite slabs. Gabe had one elbow resting on the rocks as he adjusted the focus on the scope, searching the distance for their route of travel.

"See anything?" asked Ezra, curious what was taking his friend so long to scope the countryside.

"Lots of rough country," declared Gabe, slowly scanning from the river canyon across the flats. "I figger we'd go to the Missouri an' follow it downriver till we came to a tradin' post. We know there's posts by the Mandan villages, at least that's what Munier said when we visited his post by the Poncas. The ones at the Mandan villages are also forts of Clamorgan's company, what was the name of it," he paused, trying to remember when Ezra said, "Company of Discoverers and Explorers! I remember cuz I thought that's what we were doin', discoverin' and explorin'."

Gabe turned back to look at his grinning friend then extended the scope to him, "Have a look. I figger to keep to the northeast and go 'tween that long white-capped ridge and the canyon."

Ezra put the scope to his eye, focused it then answered, "Yeah, I see it." He brought the scope along the canyon rim, across the rugged scarred country to the west of the canyon and back closer in to where they were. He lowered the scope, looked at Gabe, "You're right about that bein' some mighty rough country. We won't make much time crossin' that." He took another look around, saw something that caught his eye, then twisted around and lifted the scope for a closer look. He let out a long breath, muttered a whispered, "I don't believe it." He turned to Gabe, handed the scope and said, "Take a look down there, along the edge of that smaller canyon that feeds the big river. They just came outta that ravine yonder and are comin' this way."

Gabe lifted the scope, focused in on two riders, both leading pack horses. He dropped the scope and looked at Ezra, "Is that…?"

"Ummhmm. That's Beauchamp and the Mandan scout, Crow's Heart."

Gabe lifted the scope again, watched the two riders kick their mounts to a canter, looking back over their shoulders often. He moved the scope and saw five others, he guessed them to be Crow warriors, coming out of a ravine further back. There were two run-off creeks that scarred the flats near one another. The further one was deeper and with sides more difficult to surmount, and the closer one that was a more shallow gulley. The Indians had come from the deeper of the two and dropped into the second. By the action of Beauchamp, they had apparently spotted their pursuers and were attempting an escape.

The raider and Mandan were coming directly toward Gabe and company but were a little over two miles away. There was also a sizable draw they would have to cross before coming to the ridges where Gabe and his friends were stopped. Gabe looked below, "They'll have to cross that draw to make it to the flats out yonder. If we can get down there, we might just discourage 'em a little, ya think?"

Ezra grinned, stood and started back to their cook fire and the women, and with a quick glance back to Gabe who was putting the scope back in the case, "Well? You comin' or ain'tcha?"

Gabe chuckled, "I'm comin'!"

Within moments the two men were at the fire, explaining to the women what they planned and not surprisingly, both women insisted on coming along. Everyone had their rifles and accouterments as well as pistols and a fresh supply of determination and an eagerness for retribution.

They left the packhorses at the camp, mounted up and started to the edge of the ravine below them. Gabe placed them like a general mounting his troops. Ezra was at the end, and about thirty yards apart came Dove, Otter and then Gabe. They tethered their horses behind them, took a position near the edge of the north bluff that bordered the ravine. The bottom of the gulch was about two hundred feet below the edge, and with scattered piñon and juniper along the bank, it would not be easy for the two fleeing men to find a trail that led to the top to make their escape, but Gabe had already spotted the most likely slope and waited for the two to give it a try.

Within moments they saw the dust cloud of Beauchamp and the Mandan running their horses all out, laying low on the necks of the animals, searching the rim for a way down into the bottom and hopefully a trail up and out. Gabe saw the Crow warriors, also at a run and closing the distance between them. He looked at the white man and saw him point his horse over the edge and force the horse to take the steep slope, lunging, dropping his rump to slide, and skidding to the bottom dragging the pack horse behind. Beauchamp looked at the opposite bank, frantically searching for an easy slope up and out, saw a shoulder that looked possible, and slapped his legs to the already lathering horse, and started up. Gabe whistled his three toned screech of a red-wing blackbird, recognized by his friends and they came closer.

Beauchamp was closely followed by the Mandan and both men were merciless with their horses, kicking and slapping, whipping with the ends of the reins, forcing them to lunge, dig, and lunge again to make it to the top of the rim. But just as Beauchamp's horse made the flat, Gabe reached out and grabbed the rein, pulling the horse's neck around and dropping the animal on its side, spilling Beauchamp in a heap on the rocks. Before he could move, two rifle muzzles stared at him from the hands of Otter and Dove, daring him to try to rise. Wolf stood beside Otter, eyes slits, fangs showing as he growled threateningly. Beauchamp saw the black wolf for the first time and scooted back away, holding his hands before him as if to stop the attack of the predator of the plains.

Ezra had waited for Crow's Heart and stopped him with a wide swing of his war club that unseated the scout, dropping him flat of his back in a patch of prickly pear cactus. The scout instinctively jumped clear of the cactus, screaming his agony and grabbing at the long spines that covered his back. He saw Ezra staring at him with hate-filled eyes, holding his war club ready, watching as he picked at the painful barbs.

Beauchamp saw the women, then glanced toward the downed Mandan and saw Ezra. He turned toward his scrambling horse and saw Gabe for the first time. Gabe said, "So, we finally meet. I'm known as Gabe, but the Shoshone call me Spirit Bear, and you took my woman, Pale Otter." Beauchamp tried to roll to his knees and get up but was stopped by Otter, "You move anymore, and you will have a big piece of lead to dig out of your gut!"

Beauchamp looked from Otter to Gabe and pleaded, "You gotta let us go! There's a war party of Crow chasin' us!"

Gabe grinned, "Ummhmm. He's a friend of mine and I thought we'd save him havin' to chase you all over the country."

"Friend?! Them Crow ain't friends with no white man!" whined Beauchamp.

"Not when you raid their villages and kill their women and children and ransack what's left. Now, you're about to get what they have been plannin' for you. I don't think they were too happy that we didn't leave any of your friends for them to have their way with, so . . ." he shrugged and looked across the ravine to see the Crow drop into the bottom, coming hard and fast toward where they waited.

Spotted Crow crested the rim first, saw Gabe and drew up, but was crowded by Strikes Twice and the others. They looked at Gabe and the others and at Gabe's nod, Spotted Crow stepped down. "Spirit Bear, we meet again."

"Good to see you Spotted Crow. We saw you chasin' these two and thought we'd hold 'em for you," replied Gabe.

Crow frowned at the white man, "Are these your captives?"

"No, they're yours," chuckled Gabe.

Beauchamp screamed, "You can't turn us over to them, they'll kill us!"

Gabe answered Beauchamp, "If you can convince those women to let you go, we'll do it!" nodding toward Otter and Dove.

The women laughed, "No!"

"But, but, you don't know what they'll do!" sniveled Beauchamp.

"I think they do," answered Gabe. "That's why they're so willing to turn you over to the Crow. From what they tell me, these fellas have a way of tying you spread-eagled 'tween two trees and then shooting little bitty twigs so they just stick in you, then they set 'em on fire and watch 'em burn down. Then they build a fire underneath you and see how long you'll go without screaming. But, since you're screamin' already, I guess they won't have to do that."

As Gabe spoke, Otter translated for the other Crow warriors which were having a good laugh at the whining and screaming Beauchamp. When they looked at the Mandan, on his knees and picking at the barbs, they motioned to Spotted Crow and at his nod, caught the two horses and the pack horses, then tied the Mandan's hands behind his back, barbs and all, and lifted him to straddle his mount then tied his feet together under the horses belly.

When they started for Beauchamp, the man fell

to his face, bawling and whimpering, begging, but they jerked his hands behind him and tied him tight. Spotted Crow looked at Gabe, turned his back to Beauchamp, "We do not do what you say. We give them to the women and they beat them and make slaves of them. His life will be that of a slave. What the women do is worse than what you say."

Gabe chuckled, "I know. Otter explained that to me, but he does not know that."

Crow looked at Gabe and let a slow smile split his face. He turned to his warriors, nodded, and they threw Beauchamp belly down across his horse and used a long-braided rawhide thong to tie his feet together and stretched the long loop under the belly of the horse and around Beauchamp's neck.

Spotted Crow turned to Gabe, stretched out his arm and the two men clasped forearms. He looked at the women and Ezra, nodded and mounted. With a wave to his men, the group started down the slope of the ravine to return to their village. It would be a three-day jaunt, but they would keep their captives alive for the rest of the villagers to exact their torture and revenge for the many lives that had been taken by the raiders. As they climbed the far slope of the ravine,

Beauchamp could still be heard whimpering.

It was relief that painted the faces of the four as they sat by the small fire partaking of the meal of strip steaks and more. When the women poured cups of the chicory blend, the men sat back, glassy eyed, thinking. Ezra turned to Gabe, "We ain't on any schedule, so, how 'bout we stay right here a few days, do a little huntin', rest up, and take it easy?"

Gabe glanced at the expectant faces of Otter and Dove, then grinned and nodded his agreement. "I think all of us could use some rest," then dropping his hand to Wolf's scruff, added, "How 'bout you, Wolf? Want some kick back time?" The black fur ball looked up at Gabe, tongue lolling and answered by licking his hand. "Then, I guess it's unanimous!"

The women smiled, Otter came to the side of her man and sat down, slipped her hand around his arm and leaned on his shoulder, "It is good to be together again. I thought I had lost you when the Mandan returned with your knife. They said they killed you and saw your body float down the stream."

"Well, they sure tried. That reminds me, how 'bout checking that bandage back there?" He turned away from her and started lifting his tunic, but not before she saw the cut and tear in the back. She caught her breath at the sight of his dried blood and when he lifted the tunic to show the makeshift bandage and poultice, she carefully pulled it away to see the wound made by the thrown knife. She ran her fingers lightly over the scab, looking at the redness, then said, "You did well, it is healing properly. Was this all?"

"Uh, no." He removed his hat to show the gouge over his ear, then pushed down his britches to show the wound at his hip. Both showed pink around the scabbing but were healing well and Otter touched each once tenderly. Gabe explained, "I took the knife in the back while I was guttin' an elk. When I stood up, that's when the big man shot me in the head. It knocked me out and back into the creek. I thought I was dead, till I woke up on the sandbar. I don't know when I got this 'un," pointing to his hip.

"I heard the big man say he shot you as you floated away."

Gabe frowned, "What happened to him, anyway? I didn't see him at the camp where you were."

"We took the bad pass trail at night and his horse

fell and he went into the canyon. He was a bad man and would have hurt me and Dove."

Gabe looked at his woman, slowly realizing the trauma she and Dove had experienced at the hands of the raiders. Even though they had not been assaulted, the treatment and threat of worse had to be traumatizing. He reached out to cover her hand with his, "I'm sorry you had to go through that. I should have been more careful."

"It is over now. I am happy with you," clarified Otter, leaning against him.

For three days, the two couples lazed around, or what they deemed to be indolent or relaxing. The men hunted in the early morning, and throughout the day assisted the women as they tended the hides and smoked the meat. The spring water that served as their supply of water for themselves and the horses was little enough, but the women sent the men on a hunt and when they returned, the women had bathed, washed their hair, and wore fresh dresses and leggings. They happily welcomed the men back but pointed them to their fresh buckskins and nodded toward a small pool in the ravine below. The message was clear, and the men brokered no argument, knowing a good bath was needed. When they returned, Otter and Dove were pleased with the results, both men had trimmed their whiskers, Gabe more than Ezra, but he still had a face full, but the whiskers about his neck were trimmed and his hair was clean and the long curls tucked over his ears. Otter smiled as she went to him, reaching up to run her fingers through his hair and over his whiskers, "I like." Gabe drew her close and kissed her, and she drew him even closer.

Dove was less bold, but she too expressed her happiness at the new look of her man. Where before his thick hair looked more like a hovering storm cloud, now it was trimmed close to his scalp and his whiskers barely covered his face. She stroked his cheeks, looked closely at the hair and cupped his face in her hands and kissed him. Ezra wrapped his arms around her and held her tight as he kissed her back. The women had an exceptional meal waiting for them, fresh broiled venison steaks, a vegetable medley of cattail shoots, turnips, onions, and yucca sprouts. They had fresh strawberries, raspberries, and chokecherries for their desert.

"Eatin' like this makes me want to just stay here and get fat!" declared Ezra, grinning at Dove.

"It's been a while since I ate like this, that's for sure and certain," replied Gabe, smiling at his woman, who nodded and smiled at his back-handed compliment. "But, I reckon we need to be on the move in the mornin', if we want to make it to the trader's and back 'fore snow flies." Gabe went glassy eyed as he looked at the fire. Ezra noticed, but chose not to ask, yet he knew there was something weighing on his friend and he would share it in his own time.

But come morning, Gabe was more intent on spending some time with the Lord atop the white capped ridge behind the camp than he was about taking the trail to find a trader. He had climbed the ridge before first light, taking Wolf along, and the two sat atop the ridge, watching the sun rise and paint the sky with its usual palette of colors. He had been a little melancholy of late and needed the time to consider what had been mulling around in his mind. It wasn't homesickness that bothered him, but he was thoughtful about his sister, wondering how she was doing with her new husband and home in Washington. He also thought of his father and the last wishes of the man for Gabe to take his inheritance and follow his dreams. But his dreams did not include a massive fortune but rather the wealth of the wilderness in both exploring and discovering, not just the riches of the uncharted lands, but the treasures that were stored within himself that needed discovering and sharing. But his father had instructed their family attorney to liquidate his estate and make it available for Gabe to use as he saw fit, with minimal regard for his sister, who would be well provided for by her husband, who was heir to a sizable fortune himself.

His thinking regarding going to the trader was to send a letter to the attorney in Philadelphia to transfer the funds to a bank in St. Louis, the new French settlement at the confluence of the Missouri and the Mississippi rivers, making it more available to him if it was needed. Not that he anticipated any need that could not be met by the resources available in the mountains, as he and Ezra had learned. But he was hesitant to make his presence known in the settlement, because of the bounty that had been placed on his head by the father of Jason Wilson, the man he killed in the duel back in Philadelphia. No one knew where he was now and even if they did they would play hob to find him, and he was not anxious to make himself known to instigate a renewal of the chase and search for the bounty that the last he heard was several thousand dollars, a considerable fortune for anyone.

As he watched the blue of the morning sky chase away the last of the darkness, he dropped his eyes to the flats that spoke of the land beyond, the Missouri River and the different peoples that they had yet to meet. Then movement. Riders coming from those flats and following the river that echoed from the deep canyon. He slipped the brass telescope from the case, lowered himself to his belly and stretched out the scope to have a better look at the visitors.

Two men, dark buckskins, heavy beards, thick

hair, men that had been in the mountains for some time, perhaps Voyageurs or Coureur des bois like the raiders. They were trailing three heavily laden packhorses, probably pelts. Both men rode with long rifles laid across the pommels of their saddles, and they rode easy, using the lay of the land and any trees or rocks for cover whenever possible. They were mountain savvy and careful, but that did not mean they were a threat, nor did it mean they would be friendly. They appeared to be men long away from any vestige of civilization but were bound somewhere with their load of furs.

Gabe ran his fingers through the scruff of Wolf, then replaced the scope in the case, rolled away from the rocks and picked up his rifle and Bible and started back down the slope to the camp, staying well covered by the few trees that dotted the slope. When he trotted into the camp, his expression told of possible danger and Ezra jumped to his feet, snatched up his rifle and asked, "What is it?"

Gabe stopped, put his hands on his knees sucked air to fill his empty lungs, then answered, "Visitors!"

"Where? How many?" implored Ezra.

"Just two, trappers they look like, but . . ."

"Yeah, but! Could be raiders like them others!"

Gabe stood, shook his head, "I dunno. Could be, but they look like they've been in the mountains a long time. They're trailin' some packhorses that look like they're loaded with furs or pelts, but, well, we can either hope they miss us, or we can stop 'em."

"I'm for stoppin' 'em. I don't like anybody bein' around that I don't know all about. I've had enough of that," explained Ezra.

The women were silent, but concern was written on their faces. Gabe looked at Otter, "You two get your rifles, stay out of sight. We'll confront 'em down below and if they're all right we'll bring 'em up for some food. But if not, we'll send 'em on their way. You can watch us from the slope, there," pointing with his chin at the rise that shielded their camp from being seen from the valley floor. Gabe nodded at Ezra and the two started down the low defile that led to the lower ravine that would prompt the visitors to stop and find a way through or around. That was their choice for the confrontation.

33 / Resolution

When riding in unfamiliar country, the inclination is to take the high ground, but if the high ground has no cover, you are exposing yourself for anyone or anything to see you before you see them. So an experienced man will choose the route that does not expose him to any more than is necessary, but always ride easy and wary. The two visitors wisely chose to take the dry creek bed at the bottom of the shallow draw, believing it would lead them to a possible crossing of the deeper ravine.

Gabe and Ezra lay in wait, Gabe behind a pair of scrub piñon that clung to a rocky outcropping, and Ezra below the finger ridge that rose opposite of Gabe, leaving the trail at the bottom and riders exposed. But without any reason to expect an ambush, the men would follow the obvious game trail that led to the water in the bottom of the bigger ravine.

As they neared, Gabe motioned for Ezra to stay below cover and Gabe spoke up, "That'll do. Just sit easy and talk. Don't get too friendly with those rifles."

The men reined up at the first word, and when Gabe instructed them, the man in the lead, spoke up. "We're sittin' easy, but what'chu wanna talk about?" He was a big man, deep chested and full whiskers, dark eyes that peered from under thick brows. His broad shoulders stretched the fringed buckskins tight and the color of the skin told of many times at the campfire wiping greasy hands on chest and legs. His partner, though smaller, was wiry and still, eyes moving about and missing nothing. His badger skin cap sat at a cocky angle that hinted at a bald pate. His hands rested on the pommel of his saddle, the long rifle resting on his thighs.

"What you're doin' here," queried Gabe.

"Well, that might take a spell, we've been gone from this country for a while, and we're on our way to find a trader or someplace where we can cash in on our pelts." He paused a moment, then asked, "If'n you don't mind, how's 'bout lettin' me light my pipe?"

Gabe looked at the man through squinted eyes, wondering just how he was going to light a pipe with no fire nearby. "Go 'head, but take it slow, I'm a little nervous and my finger tends to get a little itchy at times," explained Gabe.

The man reached into his tunic, brought out a

pouch and pipe, then leaned back as he poked the tobacco into the bowl, and asked, "You gonna make us sit here all day, or you gonna invite us for coffee, that is if'n you got some. We been out for over a year now."

Gabe thought a moment, then asked, "What about you, there in the back, what do you have to say?"

"Nothin' he ain't already said," added the man.

Gabe asked the man just to hear him speak. The raiders had all been French Canadian and spoke with an accent, but these men neither looked nor sounded like the Coureur des bois. "What's your names?"

The first man answered, "I'm Michael O'Grady, they call me Irish, and my friend there's Smitty, and his name is," the man frowned, turned in his saddle to speak to his companion, "Just what is your name Smitty?"

"Hummph, it's Bartholomew Aloysius DeSmit!"

"No wonder they call you Smitty!" answered Irish. He turned back to face Gabe as Gabe answered, "I'm Gabe, called Spirit Bear by the Shoshone."

"And your partner yonder behind the ridge?" asked Irish, chuckling.

"Ezra, or Black Buffalo," came the answer from behind the ridge.

"So, now that we know each other, how 'bout that coffee?"

Gabe stepped out from behind the rocks, nodded

to Ezra and said, "You fellas just step down, empty the pans on those rifles, and we'll go have something that's as close to coffee as you're gonna get in these mountains."

Both men chuckled, appreciating the caution of Gabe and did as he bid by first flipping the frizzen forward and dumping the pans of their rifles, blowing out the remains, then snapped the frizzens closed and stepped down. Gabe led the way, and Ezra followed. As they walked into the camp, the men saw the women walk down from the rise that shielded the camp, saw their rifles and chuckled, but when Wolf came from behind Otter, both men did a stutter step back as they stared. Irish asked, "These the Shoshone that gave you those names?"

Gabe chuckled, "No, their people did some time ago." He pointed with his chin, "Have a seat." Once the men were seated and their rifles placed on the rock beside them, Gabe leaned his rifle against the log and sat down beside Ezra, facing the men. Wolf was pacing back and forth, staring at the men, head lowered slightly and showing his teeth, a behavior that any man of the wilderness would recognize as an animal anticipating an attack. Otter motioned Wolf away and the women served all the men plates full of food and cups of the chicory blend. All the men busied themselves with eating rather than talking and the visitors cast nervous glances to the edge of the trees where Wolf had bedded down. But once the plates were empty, everyone sat back to enjoy the black brew and Irish said, "Well, it ain't coffee, but it's better'n what we been drinkin'."

"So, what brought you to the mountains?" asked Gabe.

Irish, the bigger of the two men with a dark red beard and long hair, stroked his moustache, and began, "We started out with the Missouri Company," and was interrupted by Ezra who asked, "That the one they called the Company of Discoverers and Explorers?"

Irish nodded, "Yup, that's the one. See, the Spanish offered a big reward for the first expedition to reach the Pacific Ocean via the Missouri river, and Truteau and Lecuyer tried it and failed. So, James MacKay and John Evans mounted an expedition, that's the one we joined, and started out to try to get to the Pacific. We camped at Fort Charles in '95, then started again in '96. We made it to the Mandan villages, but MacKay and Evans were too concerned about makin' maps instead of exploring. They stayed there and a handful of us, six in all, decided to keep goin'." He paused and took a long drink of the steaming chicory. Then continued, "They'd talked to some Frenchies that told 'em about the Roche Jaune river, or the Yellowstone, but they couldn't find out about anything past there. So, we kept goin' on from there. For quite a spell, we

were in Assiniboine country and they was friendly
enough, but the river forked and we took the north
branch, the French call that the Milk River. That
took us into Gros Ventre country, and they weren't
too friendly, but then we were in Blackfoot country,
that's where we lost the rest of our crew. And if you
know anything about the Blackfoot," he looked at
Gabe who was nodding his head in understanding,
"then you know that's not healthy for a white man.
But at the headwaters of the Milk, we were in the
land of the Kutenai, and we made friends with them.
We spent the last two winters and one summer with
'em, trapped some of the prettiest country we ever
did see, streams loaded with beaver and mountains
with sheep, goats, elk, moose, and more." He grinned,
remembering their home of the previous two years,
then added, "But the Flathead and Blackfoot neither
one was too happy with the Kutenai and we decided
we had worn out our welcome so we decided to
skedaddle while we still had our hair."

"So, why come down this way?" asked Gabe,
suspicious of their story.

"Couple reasons. Main reason is we heard the
Yankton, Arikara and Sioux were rising up against
white men coming into their lands and were killin'
'em all. Then, we spent too much time up north
in the cold country and we got to thinkin' about
the Missouri. Comin' up, we saw many rivers that

emptied into the Missouri from the west, so we thought we'd see if we could find a better way and warmer way to get our furs to the buyers. We heard there's some folks in St. Louis that's buyin' furs and thought we'd try for there."

Gabe nodded, glanced at Ezra, "There's two. The Platte and the Niobrara. The Niobrara starts in Cheyenne country, and the Platte is sort of the dividin' line between the Cheyenne, Sioux, and the Arapaho. But both empty into the Missouri."

Irish looked at Smitty, grinning, "See, I told you we'd find us a better way!" He turned back to Gabe, "Which is best?"

Gabe shook his head, looked at Ezra and nodded. Ezra said, "We came a ways on both of 'em. The Niobrara takes you through Sioux, Ponca, and Omaha country, the Platte through Pawnee and Arapaho."

"You fellas goin' back that way?" asked Smitty. "Maybe we could go together?"

Gabe grinned, "No, we've no plans to go back." He turned to look back to the Absaroka range, "There's too much country for us to see."

The two visitors knew it was not an accepted practice to ask a man about his past and they dropped their eyes for they too had their secrets. Then Irish asked, "If you were to go, which route would you choose?"

"We made friends among several of the tribes, but if you could avoid the land of the Brule and Oglala, both Sioux, then do it. The Pawnee can be friendly or not, but we made friends with them," suggested Gabe, glancing at Ezra who was nodding in agreement.

They spent the next couple hours talking about the times spent in the mountains, the country each one saw and trails followed. When the visitors asked about the best route to find the Platte, Gabe directed them to follow the Wind River into the valley, then cross to the Sweetwater which would lead to the Platte. The men emptied the dregs from their cups and started to rise when Gabe asked, "If you fellas are goin' to St. Louis, would you be willing to post a letter for me?"

"Of course, of course. Glad to be a help. Family?" asked Irish.

"My sister. Been concerned about her, she was gettin' ready to get married 'fore I left and wanted her to know we were fine and have her answer," explained Gabe.

Ezra grinned, "Now that's an idea. How 'bout I send one along too?"

The men agreed and accepted a refill on their chicory as they waited for the men to pen their letters. It was a task, although Gabe had some writing paper and wax, but they had to formulate some ink from the ashes and berry juice, but they were soon finished and handed over the missives. Irish glanced at them, saw Ezra's addressed to a pastor and Ezra answered his questioning look, "My father." He looked at Gabe's letter addressed to the Lawyer Sutterfield, and looked at Gabe, "He's the only one still in Philadelphia that would know where my sister went with her new husband."

The man shook his head, grinned, "Now you've got me thinkin' an' feelin' ashamed I didn't write my family. Course by now, I don't know if any of 'em is still alive." He went to his saddle bags, slipped the letters into the deep pocket, then turned back to the men, "I'll take good care of them, and post them first thing! You have my word."

"Before you go, what can you tell us about the country north of here?" asked Gabe.

Irish looked at him, breathed deep and said, "It's some of the most rugged and beautiful country I ever did see. If it weren't for the Blackfoot gettin' restless, we might have spent the rest of our days with the Kutenai."

"That reward that was offered for the route to the Pacific ocean, did anybody claim it?"

"I don't think so. I figger we went further'n anybody ever did, and ain't nobody gone past the Kutenai, far's I know. So, no. Why? You interested?" asked Irish, frowning.

Gabe chuckled, "No, not in any reward, but we are

interested in any of the uncharted territory. We've considered going further north, maybe west."

It was Irish's turn to be surprised and chuckle, "So, you're goin' where we been, and we're goin' where you been. If that don't beat all."

Gabe stepped forward to shake the man's hand, clasped his shoulder with his free hand and said, "That's all I ask," and pressed a gold coin in the man's hand. He looked at it, looked up at Gabe, and said, "Keep your top knot on!"

Gabe grinned, "And you as well."

The men rode from the camp, turned and waved, then headed south along the banks of the big river, and soon were mere specks on the distant land. Gabe looked at Ezra, then to the women, smiled and said, "How 'bout we go thataway?" pointing to the northwest and the mountains beyond.

The women smiled and Otter came close, wrapped her arms around his neck and said, "Where you go, I will go."

Dove had gone to Ezra and both looked at Gabe, Ezra said, "Well, I like that, but wherever we go, we need to keep in mind that we're gonna be needin' to get ready for winter."

Ezra was the first to respond, "Yep. And I kinda like the idea of going into uncharted territory and discoverin' and explorin', don't you?"

A LOOK AT:
UNCHARTERED TERRITORY
(STONECROFT SAGA 6)

B.N. RUNDELL KEEPS YOU COMING BACK FOR MORE IN BOOK SIX OF THE FAST-MOVING STONECRAFT SAGA.

Their dream and goal had always been to explore and discover land unknown by white men. The land that lay within the territory known as New Spain or Spanish Louisiana, land that had been known as French Louisiana and that had only known the presence of Spanish Conquistadors and a few French Voyageurs or Coureur des bois. But it was the land of mountains that stood as the pillars of Heaven itself and held many natives that had never seen the face of a white man nor that of a man of color.

But now, with their new wives, Gabe and Ezra set out to discover and explore the mountains and wild country to the north. Land that was full of mystery and tales of the natives that told of indescribable wonders. Into this journey of great discovery, came a raiding horde of Blackfoot that sought to kill, maim, destroy and take captives from lesser tribes, like the Absáalooke, Agaidika Shoshone and the Bannock. When Gabe and Ezra make friends with the Shoshone, they are caught up in the war between the peoples and the price that is to be paid, maybe more than they are willing to give.

They are determined to defend their friends, and turn aside those that would wreak havoc, but what can two men do against so many?

AVAILABLE JUNE 2020 FROM B.N. RUNDELL AND WOLFPACK PUBLISHING

ABOUT THE AUTHOR

Born and raised in Colorado into a family of ranchers and cowboys, B.N. Rundell is the youngest of seven sons. Juggling bull riding, skiing, and high school, graduation was a launching pad for a hitch in the Army Paratroopers. After the army, he finished his college education in Springfield, MO, and together with his wife and growing family, entered the ministry as a Baptist preacher.

Together, B.N. and Dawn raised four girls that are now married and have made them proud grandparents. With many years as a successful pastor and educator, he retired from the ministry and followed in the footsteps of his entrepreneurial father and started a successful insurance agency, which is now in the hands of his trusted nephew. He has also been a successful audiobook narrator and has recorded many books for several award-winning authors. Now finally realizing his life-long dream, B.N. has turned his efforts to writing a variety of books, from children's picture books and young adult adventure books, to the historical fiction and western genres.

Printed in Great Britain
by Amazon

70073418R00175